Carol
Enjoy Read
Jay Crowley
12-3-22

MAGGIE

DEDICATED

This story is dedicated to Kim Robinson.

Most all of the information and research about the arrows came from different internet sites, and Kim, who directed me where to look for the information on the airmail arrows. The airmail arrows map came from Wikipedia. This information from the sites is in quotes in the story.

Thanks to Beth Watts at Fabric Chicks for all the fun quilting information and the idea about the quilting club.

Thanks to Michelle Rittel, my partner in crime, who is Nan in the story.

I could never print anything without the eyes of Josie Leeds and my husband, Tom. Most of the photos of the airmail arrows used in the story were taken by Dreamsmith Photos.

2018 Winner

ALSO BY JAY CROWLEY

Not **Worthy – Story of Revenge**
Opal
Cabin in the Meadow
Ship in the Desert
A Selection of My Short Stories
Laura
Natalie's Adventures – Middle Grade
A Gift from Nate – A Story of A Double Lung Transplant

ANTHOLOGIES

Other Realms I & II
I Heard it On the Radio
13 Bites III & IV
Plan 559 from Outer Space MK II & III
559 Ways to Die
Free For All
The Collapsar Directive
Relationship Add-Vice
Christmas Lites VII, VIII & IX

This story is a work of fiction. Some places may be real, and some of the people. Most of the people are not real. All names and events are products of the author's imagination. Any resemblance to actual names or persons (living or dead) or activities is purely coincidental and must not be construed as being real.

Email: jaycrowleybooks@gmail.com

Facebook: Jay Crowley-Sweet Dreams Books

Amazon:https://www.amazon.com/JayCrowley

For updates on new stories and more information on the author or books; visit www.sweetdreamsbooks.com

Chapter One

Maggie McDonald celebrated her sixty-eighth birthday by receiving a drone with a video camera. What was exciting about this gift? It was something she had requested from her family. Finally, they listened! Before this day, Maggie and Yazoo, her six-year-old black Lab, would hop in the Jeep Wrangler-Sahara and wander all around the desert with an old camera taking pictures. But now it was going to be different, she had a drone! Plus, Maggie had been commissioned to do an article on airmail arrows in Nevada for a Nevada magazine. The drone will be a perfect addition to do the project.

Maggie was so excited, *it can't be that hard to operate a drone. I'm not stupid,* she laughed to herself as she held on to the drone box. She almost skipped as she took it outside of her house. Standing in her large backyard by the picnic table, she opened the box and started reading the instructions. Wow, they really overwhelmed her. But she thought, *here you go, girl, read the darn book and weep.*

"So you've got yourself a new drone. Now what?" Crap, you tell me?? *"You're probably pretty excited to start flying this thing, but the reality is that*

drones aren't something that you pop out of the box and start playing with." *Really?? Thought Maggie.* "You need to protect your investment and take your time to make sure you don't break it right after you bought it, and the best way to do that is to become familiar with the Phantom drone manual. Here is how you can safely start flying your brand new drone." *They even had pictures with a pretty girl...snickered Maggie.*

"Carefully take your drone and drone accessories out of the box. *This first step must be written for an idiot. Why would you do it any other way?"* The next step in this process is to fully charge the battery." *Maggie was thankful Pete had done that already.* "A full initial charge should take anywhere from 1 to 2 hours. Make sure to remove all packaging from the drone itself once it's out of the box. Your drone will have various plastic coverings that need to all be removed before you can begin flying it." *How stupid are some people? Really, I think I know I have to remove the plastic wrapping, thought Maggie.*

"Take a peek at your App store and download the respective app associated with your new Phantom drone."

OK, I know what that is....

"Install the battery and hit the "take-off" button. Allow your drone to perform the initial tests, it's programmed to perform. These tests will include a self-test, a rotor test, and will finally climb to about three feet off the ground and hover while awaiting a command. "

What are self-tests?? Guess I will find out, as Maggie rubbed her head.

"Your drone will initially be in a limited functionality mode, which limits speed, drone range, and altitude. Make sure to become comfortable with the movement of your drone before removing the limited functionality mode."

What in the heck is this??? Oh crap, I am going to need help sighed Maggie.

"To land your drone, guide it to the spot where you would like it to land. If, at any point, you have questions about your drone or its parts, refer to this drone owner's manual."

Oh my goodness, this was all Greek, she thought. Maybe I need lessons. Heck no, I'm smart, I'm going to wing it. Pete only bought her the best, so between everybody she knew, they will figure out how to fly this darn thing.

Maggie did everything to set up the drone-like the instruction said, when the drone was on its own, it flew like a wibble-wobble doll. *Darn, I do need lessons! This sucks! That's okay, be patient. I'll get better in time.*

Pete watched her and laughed. He knew she would figure it out eventually, after forty-plus years of marriage, he wasn't about to tell her how to do it. Pete knew better as he smiled.

Today was the day! Sitting on the bed, putting on her boots, Maggie started thinking about what she hoped to find on this trip. There's so much to see on Nevada backroads. She wanted to share whatever she found with everyone, and thanks to social media, the writing of her new book, plus writing the magazine article. She was psyched at what she would accomplish.

Maggie and Yazoo headed out to pick up her friend, Nan Morgan and Beth Watts, the three of them planned on wandering out around Boomtown looking for some airmail arrows. They hope to spend the day hiking and playing with the drone. Maggie's husband Pete was in the office busy on his computer, working on some special projects. He'd been retired for several years and was now wrapped up working with 4-H youth. He didn't have a lot of the same interests as her, which is typical of most long timed married people.

"Pete, I'm taking off now. I'll see you in about five or six hours. I have my cell phone if there's a problem. I also have the two-way radios. Dinner is in the refrig, all you have to do is throw it in the oven, at 325 about 4:30 p.m. for an hour. Talk to you later. Love ya, bye," as she ran out the door.

Pete mumbles something back, which Maggie didn't understand, but knew he got the message. Nan and Bill Morgan lived only a few streets away, so it took just a few minutes to get to Nan's house. Maggie pulled up in Nan's driveway and tooted the horn. Nan came running out with her jacket, a picnic basket, and her dog. Nan was the same age as Maggie, but thirty-pound thinner, with long brown hair. Shep was part Border Collie and Sheltie. Yazoo and Shep were the best of friends. The dogs even had playdates. Yazoo started howling when he saw Shep, with his tail hitting the seat.

"Quiet Yazoo, Shep is coming," cooed Maggie.

"Maggie, this is going to be a fun day. Hopefully, we get some great pictures," chattered Nan. "I brought some treats and wine just in case we get disappointed and need to drown our sorrows," and they both laughed as she and the dog hopped in the Jeep Wrangler.

"I'm so anxious to try this drone out and show you what I learned. However, I don't have a clue how it really works, even after reading the manual," sighed Maggie with a giggle. Nan said, "Well, I'm no better, not a clue." They both smiled and laughed. "Maybe Beth knows how," clucked Nan, "these kids today know everything."

Maggie and Nan lived in the beautiful Jack's Valley at the base of Lake Tahoe. They drove toward Gardnerville observing Carson Valley with the Sierra Nevada's on one side, which still had lots of snow on Job's Peak. The valley was green from all the spring snow runoff, it was a picture perfect sight. Maggie grew up in Nevada, and Nan grew up in the Jackson Hole, Wyoming area. Seeing they were both country girls, they loved the rural lifestyle.

Turning on Johnson Lane, they headed for the Industrial Park area. This is where they would pick up Beth, as she was at her shop, called the "Fabric Chicks." The three of them belonged to a quilting club that met there called the "Wild Stitchers." The quilting group had five ladies altogether.

Maggie pulled up in front of the store and honked her horn, out came Beth quickly with her backpack, but no dog.

"Morning, Beth, this should be a fun day," stated Maggie. Beth was the baby of the bunch at forty-two, she still had children at home as well as owning and operating the fabric store. Maggie retired about two years ago, and is now an author of mystery books and does book tours. Nan retired from the Harley Davidson Company last year. She now does beautiful woodwork for fun, plus make quilts to sell.

"Do you know how to operate a drone?" asked Nan of Beth.

"Not a clue," replied Beth, "but I can learn. You have a manual?" and laughed as she opened the door and hopped into the Jeep with the dogs. The dogs leaped to the back end of the Jeep giving Beth room.

Today they decided to head out to the Boomtown Casino, which is on the other side of Reno on I-80, going to Truckee, California. The primary goal was to try out the drone with a camera and the laptop, and most of all, try not to lose the drone. Maggie hoped the pictures would help her magazine article.

Maggie's enclosed four-door Jeep was a joy for the dogs. Pete bought it for her last Christmas, and best of all, it had the power top roof that rolled back, so they could watch the drone while driving in the desert. Yazoo and Shep loved to ride and looked out the back windows as if they were a king and queen. Life was good for all of them. This was going to be a fun adventure for them all.

Before leaving, Maggie started telling the girls about today's adventure. "Last year, I met a gentleman, by the name of Kim, who gave me all kinds of information about these giant arrows called Beacon Stations that helped guide pilots who flew early airmail flights across the nation back in the '20s."

According to Kim, "Apparently, in the early days of the US Postal Service's national airmail service, pilots had to navigate across the USA by sight alone — a task that bad weather could make extremely difficult. And so a network of towers was built, each bearing a gas-powered light for night-time visibility, and each with a large arrow-shaped foundation designed to assist daytime navigation. Many of the towers in Nevada were dismantled long ago, but a number of the concrete arrows still exist to this day," declared Maggie. "It is rumored that Charles Lindberg used the arrows to fly from San Diego, where he had picked up his plane and flew to New York. This was before his solo flight over the Atlantic Ocean in 1927. Isn't that exciting?"

According to this written information that Kim gave me, which she now read to them. *"They were built at the base of a fifty-foot skeleton towers that had a 24" or 36" rotating beacon, and in the early days, the arrows were painted Chrome Yellow. Where electricity was unavailable, they used a gas generator on the wide end of the arrow to power the beacon. The site number was painted on one side of the roof of the shed; the other side of the shed had the airway number. This would point to the next higher numbered beacon station, directing the pilot along his route. All arrows pointed east on the west-east airways and north on the south-north airways. The cement arrows were built between December 1926 and November 1932, then metal arrows became the standard."*

"Anyway, supposedly, there are the remains of one of these arrows over by Boomtown. Doesn't that sound like fun? Plus, we can practice with the drone taking pictures for my article. You ladies up for it?" asked Maggie. "Look at the copy of the map that showed the route across the country. It's cool."

14

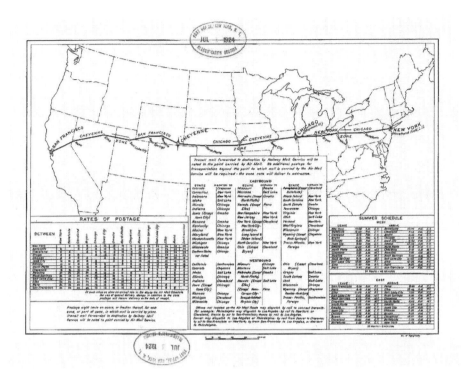

"Sounds cool, plus the beer is cold at Boomtown, plus the food is good," laughed Beth.

"I brought wine and treats to nibble on," stated Nan.

"I made us sandwiches, but a burger sounds good too," chimed

Maggie. The dogs thought the mention of food sounded good to them, as their ears perked up...

"Yep to that," said the three of them in unison as they drove off to the Boomtown area.

A couple of hours later, according to the GPS, they arrive at the site. Maggie took out the map again. "This arrow was part of the route: I would love to find more. Maybe next week we can go to the Virginia Range and see if we can find another. But, for today, let's hike up and see this one." They all agreed.

"This one is called the Mogul Arrow and is located on public land owned by the City of Reno, making it open to hiking, so anyone can go see the arrow," exclaimed Maggie.

However, for them to access the public land, they had to park in a residential area east of the arrow. After parking, they put the dogs on their leashes and started walking.

"There, that looks like the public access gate where we can hike in," advised Beth, pointing to an opening in the fence.

They hitched up their backpacks, took the drone and the dogs, and off they walked through the gate. It was not a challenging hike, but for the two old broads, Maggie and Nan, they were huffing and puffing, resting ever so often, and stopping to drink water. You would have thought they were climbing Mount Everest. Beth, being young and lean with long blond hair and beautiful blue eyes, just laughed at them as she marched up the hill with the dogs. *Darn youngster,* thought Maggie.

Nan said, "I have to quit smoking."

"That will be the day," replied Beth. Everyone laughed at that remark.

The grade was only slight to moderate, as the map said. However, it seems steep to Maggie and Nan. They probably walked less than a mile, but it felt like a ten-mile hike, with Maggie and Nan complaining all the way. They both laughed about how out of shape they were.

Maggie confided, "I have to go to the gym. This getting old is for the birds."

"I'm going with you," said Nan.

Finally, they got to the top. Maggie and Nan plopped on the ground to rest and catch their breath. Nan lit up a cigarette. It had taken them almost an hour to reach the arrow on this uphill grade. Seeing there weren't any people around to view the arrow, they let the dogs off their leash. Beth took out the drone and linked it to the computer. She got it flying, a little crooked at first, but then it straightened out. Somehow, she got it to take okay pictures. Maggie and Nan watched Beth not understanding everything she was doing.

Maggie again thought *I have to work harder on this drone thing.*

The arrow was located on a bluff overlooking I-80, with a beautiful view. The arrow pointed toward Reno. Which could be seen in the distance. The tail of the arrow pointed toward the Boomtown Casino area, only a mile or two away. Their picture was okay for a first try.

They walked the length of the arrow. It was complete, but in poor condition with numerous cracks. The yellow paint was long gone, just the gray cement color now. The arrow looks to be about fifty feet in length and maybe ten feet wide. From the information, Maggie had read, that the pilot would approach on the tail of the arrow and then exit on the head of the arrow. Maggie had also found a newspaper article on the internet site where she found the map. The newspaper article gave lots of information about the arrows. She shared the article with the girls.

"RENO EVENING GAZETTE"

TUESDAY, JULY 31, 1928

Airway Beacon Erection

Starts with First Light

To be Placed Near Mogul

**Two-Million Candlepower Lights
will Flash Guiding Fliers over Nevada;
Emergency Fields To be Lighted Also**

Erection of two million candlepower beacons, the first of the airway beacons in Nevada, started yesterday near Verdi on top of the mountain above Mogul between Reno and Verdi. A fifty-one-foot tower for the huge light was taken to the bottom of the mountain this morning by truck and with tractors, was hauled as far as the ditch which runs along the side of the mountain. Getting over the canal is a problem, the men in charge of the work said.

Twenty-six lighting units will be installed between Verdi and Battle Mountain by the San Bernardino Rock and Gravel Company. Which has the contract for this division. Six emergency landing fields between here and Battle Mountain will be lighted with the huge beacons. They will be placed on high mountains at the 225-mile division. W.W. Beanor is in charge of the work here.

The lights are controlled by an astrological clock, which turns them on at sundown. At first, a sun gauge was used on the beacons, but they were too efficient, for the beacons were turned on every time a cloud obscured the sun. Each beacon flashes a code number corresponding with the number of the beacon flash and aviators seeing the beacons flash can determine their location of landing fields in the vicinity. Where power lines are available, the beacons are electrically operated. In isolated areas, propane gas is used while others have individual power plants. The second beacon will be erected just east of the mouth of the Vista canyon on a peak above the Lockwood ranch.

Placing the beacons is a difficult job in some locations, Beanor said this morning. The parts are taken in big wide trucks as far as possible and then hauled by Caterpillar tractors. When the going gets too steep, they are loaded on sleds and hauled up by the tractor, and from then on, it's a job for the working men. At the present time, ten men are working near Verdi. Later Beanor said that there would be between twenty and thirty men on the jobs.

The first emergency landing field to be lighted will be at Fernley. On one corner, a large beacon will be built. Small fifty-watt lights will border the field at three-hundred-foot intervals. In the center of the field, a circle will be outlined in white.

The circle indicated the condition of the field. If the circle has no marks on it, then a plane can land in any direction. White lines radiating from the circles indicate the direction of a safe landing.

Within sixty days, it is expected that the beacons will all be flashing. All of the work on the Reno-Battle Mountain stretch will be completed by Thanksgiving, Beanor said."

++++++++

Finally, after an hour or so of looking around, they hiked back to the car and headed to Boomtown for a cold beer.

"That was fun and really interesting, I am going to bring my hubby and the kids up here," commented Beth.

"I'll do some more research this week to see where or even if there are more arrows in the ranges around Mound House-Dayton area. If not, we can still practice with the drone. I can tell I need lessons," sighed Maggie, and they all laughed.

Even though it wasn't hot, Maggie parked in the shade with the windows lowered, plus she gave the dog's some water and a treat. Seeing the dogs were okay, they went in to eat. Boomtown is a big Casino with Mel's coffee shop. The casino is located on the California/Nevada Border. After a nice rest and lunch, the girls headed home tired. They were excited about what they had seen and learned and were eager to share the fun information with their quilting group

Chapter Two

Every Wednesday night was quilting night from six-thirty to nine. They had been meeting for several years. Maggie always looked forward to seeing her friends. Tonight she was starting a new project. Maggie made one quilt to the other ladies three. It was an inside joke. Tonight, she decided to make a log cabin type quilt for her daughter. Usually, she did pot holders or table runners. To make a log cabin quilt patch, she had bought a dark solid color for the hearth, then lighter printed colors on one side and darker printed colors for the other side.

The hearth or the heart of the quilt will always be the darkest color. The hearth represents the home. A quilter can use any color they want, but always a dark side and a light-side. Maggie is going with a Cranberry/Rose look. Maggie cut out all the colors in three-inch strips, the width of one-half inches.

To assemble the block, you first place the strip right side against the other right side. Open and press. Turn clockwise. Add the light color strip for the second row. Then Maggie did the same way for the other rows, always turning clockwise and alternating two dark strips with two light strips. This is done until you complete the block. It seemed complicated at first, but Maggie was getting the hang of it. She hopes to make one block a week. The first one is the hardest. After that, she will just repeat the process *if I don't forget...*

The finished block should measure 7 1/4" x 7 1/4" when it is finished. However, she might have to trim it to that size. Maggie figures it will take her a while to finish the quilt as this layout needs a total of two-hundred and four blocks for the king-size quilt, which measures 102" x 88" (without borders). The quilt blocks will use about ten plus yards of fabric.

The quilt will require at least forty to fifty weeks at four-five blocks a week if Maggie makes all the blocks at a quilting class. Then the fill for the quilt is added along with the backing, plus the hand-tieing off of the quilt. She plans on having it done for her daughter. Megan's birthday in October of next year. But she thought, *as slow as I work, it might be Megan's Christmas present.*

Nan is making an Amish quilt, plus she is quite good at quilt making. She can whip a baby quilt out in a month. Her quilts sell for hundreds of dollars. Maggie laughed, *people pay me hundreds of dollars, not to make a quilt.* The evening with the Wild Stitchers is a blast, and they talk about everything. Nothing is sacred, especially when the wine flows.

Mary Normandy and Betty Santos are part of the group, Betty still works and is about the same age as Maggie. She is a cute little robust lady with dyed blond hair. Betty has lots of grandbabies, so she makes baby or couch blanket type quilts, which she also sells at craft fairs. Mary, a tiny lady in her fifties, is a widow and is the quietest one of the group. She is very soft-spoken and works at the Sheriff's Department. She loves to make quilted pillows. She gives them to family or friends for gifts. Beth is the teacher, as she owns the shop.

After a couple of glasses of wine and a lot of laughter, Maggie was wired and decided to tell the group a camping story.

"A couple of months ago, Nan and I were camping with some city-slickers. Basically, these people never lived in the country or on a ranch. Nice people, but we took them snipe hunting." Everyone laughed.

Maggie took another sip of her wine. "Yep, we told them we should all go down to the cow pasture by the RV park, where a bunch of cows was grazing and go cow-tipping."

Nan chimed in, "and they wanted to go... can you believe it???" Everyone laughed again and asked. "What did you do?"

"Well, this went on for the better part of an hour, and everyone believed they could go cow-tipping. Nan and I weren't sure what we were going do, so we told them that the next camping trip we go on, we would be prepared with flashlights, etc., for cow-tipping," explained Maggie. "It was so darn hard to keep a straight face," laughed Maggie and Nan.

"For the next month, every time we saw them, it was all they talked about. Right, Nan?"

"Yep. So we decided we better tell them the truth," stated Nan.

"They were the sorriest bunch of people you ever saw; they had been looking forward to an adventure. Can you imagine, going cow-tipping? Some old bull would have chased us right through the fence," and everyone belly laughed at Nan mainly because of the faces and gestures she made. "We had so much fun. But I don't think they'll ever believe us again, right, Maggie?"

"Probably not. But it was worth it," giggle Nan.

"It was cruel to tease them like that," grumbled Mary. "Mainly because you guys knew it wasn't true and they believed in you. Didn't you feel bad?"

"Not really, if they are that gullible," and Nan and Maggie laughed again.

"Changing the subject," Maggie snorted, "so we don't offend any snowflakes here," making a face at Mary by sticking her tongue out. "Nan, Beth and I went 4-wheeling the other day to see some airmail arrows. It was fun. We are going again to see if there are any around the Virginia Range. We brought in a blurry picture," which she placed on the table. "Trying to get the hang of the drone," divulged Maggie. "I did find some good pictures on the internet thanks to Dreamsmith photos," which she also showed them.

All the ladies looked, "wow, interesting," said Betty, "where is this?"

"This one is out by Boomtown, and you have to hike about a mile, which Nan and Maggie complained the whole way," chimed Beth with a smile.

"We did not," they said in unison. Beth just looked at them. "Well, I guess we did complain a little," coughed Nan.

"A little, for an hour and a half," Beth laughed.

"Okay, okay, we complained, but we are old," claimed Maggie. The whole group roared in laughter as they clicked their wine glasses.

"Let me explain a little about these arrows, it's quite interesting. I've done a lot of research. Scattered across Nevada in the early years of aviation, there was a network of concrete arrows. They built them because there wasn't must population in Nevada at the time. They are found in remote locations or areas that are difficult to access."

Maggie continued, "some of the arrows were accompanied with a small shack, a few had a metal tower affixed to their base. Many are still in good condition, while others have succumbed to nature or construction due to the population growth. The shape and direction of the arrows vary, but it is clear they served the purpose of assisting the pilots.

According to everything I read, the primary purpose was important: helping early pilots navigate the U.S. transcontinental with flights along with night navigation. This all occurred before radar. The pilots had to use ground-based landmarks for guidance, especially in Nevada. These beacons worked for flights during the day, but were mainly for at night.

"But like everything, technology changes," Maggie continued, "the beacons were established across the United States to guide airmail pilots, as I said before radar, as it wasn't invented until 1935 by Sir Robert Watson-Wall of England. When radar and radio communications were created, it made the beacons obsolete within a few years. Most of the beacons have been torn down or abandoned throughout the country. I understand many of the arrow markings were removed during World War II, to prevent aiding enemy bombers in navigation. But as you can see, there is still one out by Boomtown. That ladies is your lesson for the night." Maggie took a breath and a sip of wine.

"Anyway, we are going out on Friday to look for more arrows. Anyone want to come?" asked Maggie.

Mary said, "How do we know this trip you want us to go on isn't a snipe hunt like your cow-tipping story?"

"Asked Beth and look at the pictures. This is for real. Plus, you can google it on the internet," replied Nan seriously. Everyone looked at Mary and saw she was kidding and laughed.

As it was, everyone declined for one reason or another, except Nan. "Fine, we will fill you in next week on what we find."

The rest of the evening went fast with gossip and a little wine. Maggie got her first block done than three more. She was so proud. At nine o'clock, she and Nan said their farewells as the group broke up for the evening and headed home.

Nan dropped Maggie off and said, "See you Friday around ninish."

"Sounds good, I bring snacks."

"See you then, have a great night," responded Maggie. "Love ya."

"Yep, you too," as Nan hopped out of the Jeep.

Chapter Three

On Friday, Nan and Maggie drove toward Dayton and started driving towards the Como peak area. In its heydays, Como Peak was a mining camp, but now just some old ruins are left. While wandering around, they got some great camera still shots of wild horses. There was a herd of five horses roaming around. Wild horses are beautiful animals.

Some of the wild horses are feral horses that people turned loose many years ago, during the recession. People lost their homes, and they couldn't afford to feed their horses anymore, so they let them go wild. Sometimes a stallion will break down a fence and steal a domestic mare to mate. However, there are still a few pure mustangs left.

Bureau of Land Management (BLM), however, keeps gathering the wild horses up, and it has caused quite a rift with the people. Mainly it is the way they do it. They chase the horses with helicopter maiming and killing some of them.

Neither of them had used the drone on the trip. They stop for a break, giving the dogs a chance to run. Maggie started rereading the manual again on how the drone works, Beth had made it looks so easy. Finally, she managed to set up the laptop in the Jeep so she could watch the drone when it flew above the vehicle. However, it was trickier than she figured.

Maggie wasn't quite sure she was ever going to get the hang of it. It would go up and down, and side to side, she couldn't get it to stay on a stable course. Plus, it could only fly for about twelve minutes before it needed a new battery.

"Guess I'm going to have to talk to somebody," she said to Nan frustrated. "Someone who understands drones and then go out with them to really get the hang of this. Looks like today is mostly about the drone and not finding more airmail arrows."

"However, we did get some excellent camera shots of wildlife," explained Nan. They saw a young eagle, red-tailed hawks, a couple of deer, no antelope, as well as quite a few wild horses. Seeing it was still early in the morning, they decided they would drive down to the Silver Springs area and wander around for a little bit.

However, seeing Maggie really wanted to get this drone to work. She stated, "maybe we need a flatter area, with not so many trees. That way, if something happens, we won't lose the drone in a tree".

Maggie remembered there's an alkali lake out by Dayton, not too far from where they were. So they drove off to the playa. At the alkali lake, after an hour or so of playing with the drone, she got it up and had it flying pretty good. She even landed it. They were able to get some pretty good video through the computer of the dried lake bed. However, Maggie had used six batteries and only had four left.

"You know when I was a kid, there were lots of wild horses in this area. People used to chase them across this lake in their truck, rope and sell them for horse meat. Then the State finally passed laws to stop it. Now the Bureau of Land Management chases the wild horses with helicopters, corrals them, and sells them for horse meat because they are above the State law. Funny how things work," grumbled Maggie.

"What brought that on?" asked Nan.

"You know I not sure, maybe because they filmed the "Misfits" here, and it was about horse poachers," replied Maggie, "or I am hungry." With that, she called the dogs in. Shep and Yazoo were having so much fun running all over the lake bed, getting all dusty. "Come on guys, get a drink and a treat." They came on a dead run at the word treat.

After loading everybody up, they drove to a shady spot by some pinion pines and spread the grub out on the tailgate of the Jeep. They were all hungry and thirsty. Maggie had made ham and cheese sandwiches, with barbeque chips and jerky for the dogs. Nan brought some water and homemade zucchini bread.

Maggie thought *I'm going to ask my son for help. He works with a fellow who has a drone and apparently knows lots about them. Maybe he can help me understand more about this darn thing.* She should've done that before she planned this trip, but she was so excited to try to locate more airmail arrows and write the article that she didn't plan ahead. One of these days, she would get organized and laughed at herself... *really?*

After eating, they were ready to travel again. This time, they turned off a road before Silver Springs and headed north, in an easterly direction. It was a dirt road neither of them had been on before. They came to several crossroads and sometimes going to the left, mainly taking the way that looked the smoothest. The BLM maintained road got rougher as they wandered back through the desert and mountains for miles into the Virginia Range. Nevertheless, the area was beautiful. They saw deer, wild horses, range cattle, and many birds, but no sign of airmail arrows.

Around a flat area, Maggie set the drone flying, best of all, it was working through the computer darn good. The sad part it was using up the remaining batteries like mad.

"I wish I could get my hands on an excellent map of the arrows, it sure would help. I'll have to try the library," complained Maggie.

"What is that? It looks like a herd of something over there by that knoll," explained Nan looking at the computer screen.

Maggie stopped the Jeep and looked. Sure enough, there on the camera, they could see something. Nan guided the drone over toward what seemed like a herd of cows or something, to get a better look. Whatever it was, they were in a makeshift pipe and snow fence portable type corral.

"Damn it, Nan, it's horses in that corral, maybe ten or so," exclaimed Maggie, all excited, "bring the drone back, just in case there is a problem."

The horses were pacing in the corral, but thankfully, it had a gate. Both Nan and Maggie thought that it was odd. Why would there be horses corralled out here in the middle of nowhere? "This is BLM land, but this doesn't look like a BLM roundup," stated Nan.

They drove over and saw the horses had no water or feed. Though they didn't look like they'd been there very long. Maggie looked around for any signs of human life, a truck, or something. Seeing nothing, she stopped the Jeep. Everyone jumped out of the vehicle along with the dogs. They ran over to open the gate to free the horses, but they couldn't get the ropes to budge.

Maggie ran back to the Jeep and got an ax and came back. After a couple of whacks, the cotton ropes gave that was holding the gate open. When Maggie let them out, the horses started running away like mad.

Soon as Maggie had let the horses out, a shot hit the dirt by her feet, and she was like *wow!*. She looked around and starting running back to the Jeep when another shot rang out by Nan in the soil.

"Run in a zigzag pattern in the horse's dust," yelled Maggie. She called for the dogs while running to the Jeep. Yazoo, Shep, and Nan jumped into the passenger side of the Jeep, while Maggie got in on the driver side behind the wheel. Firing up the engine, she peeled out, driving zig-zag. Damn! As someone was still shooting at them.

Then it dawned on Maggie. *This must be horse poachers. Criminy, we had just been talking about them. Was she psychic or something?* Somebody was poaching the wild horses either to sell or slaughter. Who would be doing this out here? This wasn't BLM. These actually were horse poachers! Plus, Maggie had a video of the trapped horses. Maybe there were some clues on the tape as to who was behind gathering up the horses. Her mind was racing.

They headed back down the road as fast as they could. It was a bumpy dirt road and of course, no cell service because Nan tried. The two-way radios wouldn't work as they were too far out. Maggie was the only one with a gun. While she has a concealed weapons permit, Nan didn't have one. Maggie thought, *Goodness, if they follow us, what are we going to do? I don't want a shootout in the middle of nowhere.* She was distraught as she drove hell-bent for leather in the Jeep, hoping she remembered how to get out of the area. It took about thirty minutes to get back down to where they were on a smoother road. Then she could really go like a bat out of hell to get back to civilization. Thank goodness no one was following them.

Finally, Nan got cell service and called the authorities, but they didn't have a location as to where the incident occurred. Maggie and Nan were so mad at themselves for not getting a topographic description of the area. But at the time, they just wanted to get the heck out of there, since somebody was shooting at them. They told the Lyon County Sheriff Office that they would meet them in Dayton.

When they arrived at the police sub-station in Dayton, the officer checked their vehicle and found a bullet hole in the spare tire. Thank goodness, no one was hurt. The officer dug the bullet out, he could see it was from a hunting rifle, it looked like a .223, and was proof that somebody had shot at them. However, Maggie didn't have the location, but she had a video of the area.

Maggie was still angry that she didn't have a topographical description, and of course, both her and Nan were extremely upset about being used for target practice.

They walked around, heck it was more like pacing from anger while talking to the cop. The cop took the report trying to calm the gals down and get all the information, but it wasn't much help.

Maggie said, "I did save the horses. There were about ten of them. I axed the gate and got them out. Somebody up there was horse poaching, as these were apparently wild horses. These people were not happy that we showed up, and that's was why they were shooting at us. Thank goodness they were poor shots," Maggie rambled on.

The young officer whose nametag read Jefferson smiled as he took their report and the bullet. Maggie told them she would get him a copy of the video. After all of that, the women went home with a story to tell.

Maggie brought the camera into the house to show her husband the video on the laptop. He could hear the shots being fired at them, and it really upset Pete. He told Maggie, "I don't want you going out there alone again. They could've killed you, and we wouldn't have known where you were."

Maggie had to agree they never would've found their bodies. Now that the incident was over, it was scary to think about what could've happened.

Chapter Four

The next day Maggie reviewed the tapes again to try to get a feel for where the area was located. However, she had never been there before, so it was all new to her. Maggie stopped the computer to make still pictures. She ended up with about twenty different photos of the area and several of the fenced-in corral. The funny part was the drone never saw a pickup or any car, so where was the shooter's vehicle? Where were they shooting from? Maggie's mind was racing. *Why would anyone want to capture those horses? Money, of course, sell them or slaughter, either way, it was about the money. It's always about the money.*

Maggie decided to post some of the pictures on Facebook, asking if anybody recognized the area. It was worth a try, someone else may have been up there when there weren't any horses corralled. She wondered *how many times had the poachers done this? How many horses had been captured? And who were they?*

As Maggie sat there, she remembers as a kid using those types of corrals to gather cattle off the range to bring them in for the winter and for cutting calves. They were pretty common. Any rancher in the area could have them, or you could rent them. They could be loaded in the back of several pickup trucks, as they are portable. But again, who would have placed the corrals out there?

It was scary to think that they would try to kill people. Then she thought for a moment, maybe they were just trying to scare us away, which they sure in the heck did.

However, Maggie wanted to go back, regardless of what Pete said. She made a copy of the tape and pictures for Officer Jefferson. Maggie would deliver them tomorrow to the Lyon County Sheriff's Office in Dayton.

Maggie got the drone manual out again and read it for about the fifteenth time she just couldn't understand how the dang thing worked adequately. The hard part was to get it to stay stable. Plus, she didn't understand the syncing between the drone and the computer. She didn't think she was that stupid. *Gonna have to find somebody who really understands these things. It can't be that complicated. I'm just, I guess, not coordinated.* She texted her son, asking him to ask his friend Justin to give her a call. Maybe he could explain and show her how the darn thing worked. Maggie wanted to make sure she was doing it right before she went out again. Because she was going to go back to the same area of the corrals but wanted to be prepared this time.

The next day, Maggie went into Carson City to get her tire fixed on the Jeep. She wasn't sure what they could do to fix the tire since she's never had a tire shot before. Going into Discount tires, Maggie talked to the manager, who, after looking it over, said they couldn't patch it. He recommended a new tire. Apparently, the bullet going into the casing didn't do much damage, but when it comes out on the other side, it left a big hole. They felt it wouldn't be safe. So that cost her two-hundred and twenty dollars. Well, that's better than our lives or Yazoo and Shep.

She met Nan at the Red-Hut Cafe on Fairview for lunch. She loved their chicken salad sandwich, plus her granddaughter, Christa, worked there. Everyone working there had heard about the shooting from Christa and talked to them about what had occurred. Some local people stopped by their booth to ask how they were and what happened. For a few minutes, Nan and Maggie were celebrities. Little did they know that they were being observed in the restaurant, and their conversations overheard in a nearby booth.

For the next few days, Maggie tried to concentrate on doing other things around the house, but her mind kept drifting back to the shooting. I guess that's normal. One morning, while she was folding the laundry, she was thinking about what could have happened and was thankful that it hadn't happened. However, the other side of her mind was saying I need to go back there to see what is going on. If nothing else, Maggie was a stubborn Irishwoman, once she got her teeth into something and she never liked to let it go. *I don't like being shot at, even if it's just to scare me. In fact, I don't want someone scaring me at all. Dammit! What if they had shot Yazoo?* Maggie never folded clothes so fast than she did that morning, with her mind racing.

She sat down with a cup of coffee and tried to recall that day. It started out as a beautiful day going to Dayton, taking pictures, and practicing with the drone. Then she got it into her skull to go someplace where they've never been. Hopefully, to find more airmail arrows. However, they got a lot more than they bargained for, captured wild horses, and getting shot at!

On the positive side, the countryside was beautiful, the horses were gorgeous, there was so much to be thankful

44

for. In addition, they saved the horses from who knows what. But darn, someone still shot at them!

All Maggie could think about was she was angry that some idiot shot at them. The more worked up, she became, she thought *I had to find out who it was that took a shot at us. Come hell or high water.*

Chapter Five

Justin Smith was around twenty-seven and worked with her son. Maggie's son said he was good with technology and has a fancy drone. Fancy wasn't even the word, Justin's drone was about four feet in diameter with the video camera. It was the Rolls Royce of drones. He explained to Maggie how the drone worked. All Maggie heard was blah blah blah blah blah. The only thing she really understood was it would take about two weeks to learn the fine art of drone flying.

Well, let's get started, she told him. Justin said he could work with her after work three days a week until she got the hang of it. Maggie's drone was a Hubsan 107D, about half the size of Justin's. According to Justin, Maggie's drone was capable of capturing clear aerial images and comes with a reliable camera. But it was not known to be really stable. Justin said it was an excellent drone for what she wanted to use it for, which was taking pictures. It only had an air flight time of about fifteen minutes per battery. She must carry extra batteries. *She already knew this.*

What little time she had already spent with the drone, she had noticed it went through batteries fast. Thank goodness, she had ten batteries and a regular/solar battery charger.

All Maggie wanted to do was take pictures of the airmail arrows and animals and write an article for a magazine and a book showing photos of the backcountry in Nevada. However, now she also wanted to find and catch the horse poachers. Her husband wanted her to find the airmail arrows, and maybe a herd of antelope, some wild sheep, wild horses, and deer, but no poachers. He was adamant about that. She laughed to herself, *and when did I ever listen to him...*

Maybe the place to check out for the wild horses and poachers is to go back into the Virginia Range, which is almost to Fernley, she might find more airmail arrows if she's lucky. She knew she had to work around Pete, he was watching her like a hawk. He said he was going with her next time she went out into the desert. *Like she was a three year old...*

For the next few weeks, time went fast, between Maggie taking drone lessons, quilt making, and spending time researching the airmail arrows. Maggie learned a lot. She found out about the remains of a beacon out by Derby Dam outside Sparks. From the research she was gathering, the route pretty much followed I-80, so the likelihood of finding arrows in the Virginia range was diminishing.

Maggie learned that there were seventeen arrows and eight beacons in the state, many down near Las Vegas. Nevertheless, she couldn't wait to go see the one by Derby Dam near Fernley. Maggie thought, *wait until I tell the quilting group., what I learned.*

Wednesday night, she had much to say about the airmail arrows. "If I drive the motorhome, who wants to go on a trip to find these arrows and use the drone?" she asked.

"How long would we be gone?" asked Beth.

"Maybe a week, or less if we don't kill each other," laughed Maggie.

"Are you taking us, cow-tipping?" smirked Mary.

"Only you," replied Nan. Everyone laughed.

"What happened to the horse poacher? Beth asked.

"Oh, I'm still working on that little problem," quipped Maggie. "I am getting everything in order."

It seems that only Nan and Maggie were the adventurous ones. They planned on going next week, after their quilting class, in case anyone changed their mind and wanted to go. Everyone else seems to have commitments. The evening was a success. Maggie finished her twenty-fifth block. Nan completed her Amish quilt and was starting a baby quilt. Maggie thought, *smart aleck...*

Chapter Six

The following Wednesday evening, as they sat around working on their quilting projects. Betty asked, "I have been wondering about those horse poachers, wonder how they planned on getting the horses out to where ever they were taking them? They must have a large truck somewhere."

"Good question," responded Nan.

"Who do we know in the area that has a cattle truck to haul horses?" questioned Maggie.

"Yeah, but you guys aren't sure they're from this area," chimed Betty.

"Good point, but my gut thinks they're local, strangers wouldn't know the area," replied Maggie.

"Maybe we could stake out the area with cameras," suggested Beth, "you know the game hunting type.

Everybody looked at her with blank eyes, "I am not aware of these types of cameras," stated Mary.

"Sounds good, but I am not sure I can find the spot again for one, and two, where would we hide the cameras in the desert? There are no trees," declared Maggie.

"No, but from these pictures you took, there's scrub brush, and that gets pretty big," replied Beth.

"Good point," chimed in Nan.

"Maybe when we come back from seeing the airmail arrows, I will take cameras out there, if we can find the spot again," sighed Maggie.

The conversation continued. No one had the right answer or a solution to the problem. Maggie thought *the only answer was to go back out there and find the spot, but this time I will be prepared.* Maggie got another five blocks done, feeling very proud. Darn Nan was halfway finished with her baby quilt. Maggie justified it in her mind that Nan's blocks were smaller...

Maggie had mixed emotions about this trip, she wanted to find out what was going on with the horse poachers, but was curious about the airmail arrows and wanted to finish her article. So for now, the trip won out.

Thursday morning, they all headed out to locate more arrows, Maggie, Nan, Pete, and the dogs. Nan's husband Bill couldn't get the time off. Pete was driving the motorhome towing the Jeep. The first stop was the Derby Dam Beacon site located on the north side of I-80 east of Sparks, Nevada.

It was hard to get to. If Pete blinked, he would have missed the dirt road leading to the arrow. They pulled onto the shoulder behind the guardrail, and Pete disconnected the Jeep. There was a dirt road along with a closed gate, but no signs saying 'Keep Out' on the gate. The only sign on the gate said, "All the property beyond the gate is owned by the Federal Government and managed by the Bureau of Land Management." After going through the gate, Maggie jumped out of the Jeep and made sure it was closed completely.

Using the four-wheel drive, they went approximately three miles. Due to the loose rocks and poorly maintained road, they decided to hike the rest of the way to the beacon site on top of the hill and not following the road. It was a slow and tedious hike to the top, as the slope was covered with small and loose rocks. Maggie and Nan complained the whole way.

"I have got to go to the gym, I am seriously out of shape," stated Maggie breathing so hard she could hardly talk.

"I am going with you," confirmed Nan. "This hiking is killing me." Everyone laughed.

Even Pete was laboring, but the dogs thought it was fun as they ran up the hill and back. The top of the hill, where the site was located, provided an excellent view. All that was left of the beacon was in ruins, but it was still impressive. Three poles were remaining, as the buildings had been removed.

From the top of the hill, they could see the Tracy Clark Arrow. Pete and the dogs hiked down. Maggie and Nan bowed out, saying, "Uncle, these two old broads are done climbing."

Maggie copied pictures off the internet from Dreamshop Photos, which were probably better than they could have taken. After hiking around the area, they all headed back to the Jeep. It was around two, and everyone was hungry. However, all the food was in the RV. Maggie thought *I should've brought snacks, I only brought water. Darn, I never plan ahead.*

About an hour later, they arrived back at the coach, hooking up the Jeep for the next adventure, but first some food and rest. The arrow out by Lovelock will be their next stop tomorrow, so tonight they would stay at The Lazy K Campgrounds and RV Park in Lovelock. Maggie had a feeling everyone would sleep well tonight.

The dogs had them up early, as they wanted to go potty and eat. Maggie thought *it's so quiet here I could sleep longer.* Nonetheless, she got up and started the coffee. She had brought apple fritters from the local bakery in Carson. None of them were big breakfast eaters, just the dogs. Today, she thought, *I will be organized and packed some treats for the ride and hike.*

According to the information Kim gave Maggie, the Humbolt Arrow is approximately 20 miles south of I-80 out in the middle of the Nevada desert. They exited I-80 at Coal

Canyon Road, which eventually turns into Iron Mine Road. The first seventeen miles were paved. Following the directions, Maggie had received from Kim, the Internet, and their GPS, they turned left off of Iron Mine Road, parked the RV and disconnected the Jeep. They drove about two miles out to the arrow. The arrow was located on a small rise, and by using the four-wheel drive in the Jeep for the last quarter mile, they were able to drive right to the arrow itself.

"This is awesome, no hiking up giant hills today... wahoo!" shouted Nan as she hopped out of the Jeep and lit up a cigarette. Maggie looked at her and laughed. "What??" asked Nan as she took a long drag on her cigarette.

The fifty-seven-foot arrow was more complete, but in poor condition. It has multiple cracks and had broken apart. Sage was growing out of its crevices. Maggie used the drone to take a picture, mainly to get the overview effect.

Maggie asserted, "this is so great! I am so thankful for Kim, giving us this information about this piece of history. Living here all my life, I didn't know about them."

Everyone had to agree. They spent a good couple of hours hiking around the arrow and admiring the scenery. Nevada has a beauty of its own. However, even with all of this going on, Maggie wondered about the horse poachers. *Wondering how many more horses they had captured, seeing it had been almost a month since the incident.*

That night at dinner, they discussed their plans for tomorrow.
Maggie talked about another arrow, "according to the internet, not much remained of this one. It's located at Polkinghorne Springs in Pershing County."

Everyone decided they would pass on that one. The next one coming up was Buffalo Valley Arrow outside of Battle Mountain, further east on I-80. They planned on visiting that one tomorrow.

"Who knew all these arrows existed," drawled Pete. "You could travel the whole state just looking for the airmail arrows. They are fascinating. I wish they still worked."

"I wish Bill could have come with us, I know he would have enjoyed this trip." chimed Nan.

The conversation continued on about what they had seen and the ones left to see. Finally, everyone was tired, especially Yazoo and Shep, who had been snoring throughout the conversation. Tomorrow was another day.

Chapter Seven

Everyone was up early, and Maggie had the coffee on with what was left of the sweet rolls placed on the table. They knew to reach this arrow would take some traveling.

Around ten in the morning, they arrived and parked the motorhome at the Broadway Flying J RV Park in Battle Mountain and disconnected the Jeep. Maggie had packed lunches this time and plenty of water.

To reach the Wild Range Canyon/Buffalo Valley Arrow, they drove south on Hwy 305 out of Battle Mountain for about eleven miles by the GPS and turned right onto Copper Basin Road. There was a street sign at the intersection, making it easy to find.

From that intersection, it was about a twenty-one-mile drive across the desert to the arrow. The first two miles were paved, while the next nineteen miles were a hard-packed gravel road. After going twenty miles, Pete made a right turn onto a narrow dirt road saying, "crap, this resembles more of a cattle path than a road. Hang on to your bra straps, it looks rough."

The GPS is a blessing out here to locate the arrow because once you turn on the gravel road, you could get lost with all the crossroads and no signs.

However, the trip was worth it, as the Buffalo Valley Arrow was complete and in good condition. The arrow was about fifty-seven feet in length. In her excitement, she had forgotten the drone, but Maggie had downloaded a picture from the internet.

There were lots to see with this arrow, especially where the old beacon house stood. There was no one there, except for a couple of coyotes off in the distance. Maggie let the dogs run for a bit, then put them back in the Jeep. Coyotes are known to attack dogs. They saw some wild horses in the distance, and again, Maggie wondered about the poachers.

It was around two when they arrived at the arrow, so they were hungry. Putting the tailgate down on the Jeep, they had lunch.

"I think this is the best arrow so far," declared Nan.

"Sure has the most remains, so you can see how it all works," disclosed Pete.

"I wish I hadn't forgotten the drone, but the internet gave us some great aerial photos," signed Maggie. "Plus, I need to get better at handling it in the wind."

"You will get the hang of it, Hon, just give it time," chirped Pete.
They all laughed, and Maggie stuck her tongue out at them. It was a great day, so much to see and being with good friends.

That evening at dinner, they planned the next day trip. They would be traveling further east to Wells and staying at the Angel Lake RV Park.

The following day was a repeat of the last two. Maggie made coffee, but today, they had peaches for breakfast. Maggie made lunches for later as they headed out to Wells. Soon as they parked the RV, Pete disconnected the Jeep and set the GPS for the trip.

The Welcome Arrow is located out in the desert just off of I-80, west of Wells, Nevada. The arrow is in poor condition and partially covered with sagebrush. The arrow point itself is broken-up and is also located between two microwave towers surrounded by a chain-link fence. The arrow is around fifty-three feet in length. This made it hard to fly the drone, not wanting to hit a beacon. Maggie again got the pictures off the internet.

Maybe it was because they had seen so many arrows, that this one didn't seem to interest them as much as some of the others. So they didn't spend much time here, ate their lunch while the dogs ran, then headed back to camp. They didn't see any wildlife. The next tower was in Elko County.

The beacon tower at the Little Lake Pass which is in Elko County. This site would be their last stop as they had to start heading home. Parking their RV at Iron Horse RV park as Little Lake is a pass out in the middle of nowhere. Using the Jeep and their GPS is the only way they would be able to find it. But, everyone said it is worth the try.

The site is no. 49-A on the San Francisco-Salt Lake Airway map. It is located on a jutting outcrop at 6,860 feet above sea level. The caretaker's dwelling nearby is at an altitude of 6,750 feet. According to the internet information, Kim gave Maggie, "During winter, the site sometimes is blockaded against normal vehicle traffic for as much as four months at a time, and at its worst, snowshoes are the only available means of getting to and from the station because of massive snowdrifts.

Ordinarily, a light beacon site does not have a full-time resident caretaker, but is serviced during periodic inspection visits. In the event of light failure, a special trip is made to the site. At Little Lake Pass, however, and at the few other similarly inaccessible beacon lights, a caretaker lives at the site to maintain and service the light. He also has the responsibility for different lights in the vicinity. Certain

Stations on the Federal Airways System, usually known as intermediate landing fields, are noncommunication stations because they're not equipped with a radio or teletypewriter. The Little Lake Pass beacon site can indeed be called a noncommunication station, for it does not even have a telephone. The nearest beacon site to 49-A is site number 50, Silver Zone. The tower there is 6,490 feet. The dwelling is 6,300 feet above sea level and about seventeen air miles distant from the site no. 49A."

Pete stated after reading, "so, this is a real remote arrow."

The information further reads, "The keeper in charge at 49-A made a request to his mechanic for some sort of signal light so that in the event of urgent need, a signal could flash out to the keeper in charge at site 50. The request was granted. The mechanic arranged for a signal light at site 50 also. So the keepers in charge could flashback an acknowledgment back and forth. In October of 1934, these lights were installed. They were 500-watt course lights with red lenses.

It was understood that 49-A, in the event of necessity, would flash his red light and leave it on. Then 50 would flash an acknowledgment as soon as he had seen it.

If there were an urgent need of 49-A, he would merely leave his light on-and the keeper at 50 would come over as soon as he could. If the case could wait until morning, then 49-A was to flash four times. As of the present, there has been no need for sending out such a signal, which would have been a red one.

But the idea of sending out an okay signal once a week with just a white light was agreed upon. This was done by merely raising the red lens out of the way. When only the white light was showing, it was understood just a message was being sent out. As the road up to the station is steep and rather narrow there is a possibility of something going wrong on the way up, so the keeper, when he visited the town or returning to his station, flashes a signal to the people at Shafter, signaling his safe arrival at the station after his beacon has started.

The Morse code is used for Shafter because it is understood there. With a light, the dot is a short flash, and the dash is longer in duration. But only short signals previously agreed upon have so far been put to use between the two airway stations. As a rule, an okay is sent out each Saturday evening just to let it be known all is well at 49-A."

"Dang, that's interesting. Because these arrows were so remote, if there had been a major problem or illness, the keeper could have died before help could get to him," commented Pete.

It took them most of the morning to arrive at the Little Lake Arrow, but well worth seeing.

Little Lake Pass #49A

The girls were through, but Pete wanted to make one more stop at the Silver Zone Pass seventeen miles away. As it turned out, of all the arrows they visited, this would be their favorite.

However, just to reach the base of the path to the arrow, they had to drive approximately five miles on the dirt - gravel road, part of which was a 'washboard.'

Nan said, "tighten your bra straps again, we are in for one heck of a ride." As they bounce all over the seat of the Jeep, even the dogs were having trouble.

The last half mile they had to use 4-wheel drive, due to the road being uphill on loose shale. They went as far as they could, then they had to get out of the Jeep and hike up the hill. That had to be done slowly. Which was okay by the girls as they panted up the hill. They all had to be cautious due to the loose shale. Of course, the dogs ran around like they were mountain goats.

The Silver Zone Pass is a completely intact 90° arrow. The view from the top of the mountain was incredible, as the air was clear and clean. They could see for miles. It was late afternoon when they reached it, which just enhanced the colors and shadows. In the very far distance, Maggie could barely make out I-80. The first two parts of the arrow, as it is a five-part arrow is located on an uphill slope. The middle portion of the arrow, where the beacon stood, is on level ground. While the next two pieces of the arrow are on a downhill slope. A small part of each of the beacon tower legs remains embedded in the arrow. This was an exciting arrow as it has a curve.

The elevation was high at the top of the mountain, and Pete made a comment, "Wow, it's chilly," as he rubs his shoulders and hands.

Nan replied quickly, "You got a spoon?"

Pete looked at them quizzically, and both gals broke out laughing.

It was after four when they headed back to Elko, and this was their last night. Maggie thought *I'll be glad to be heading home tomorrow.* So tonight they would celebrate. They decided to have dinner at the "Star," a Basque restaurant, with outstanding food and great pecan punches, which is a Basque drink.

Maggie thought *now that we are heading home, I can concentrate on those poachers.* She hoped Pete would forget about her traveling in the desert and be busy with his 4-H stuff. But for tonight, we are going to have fun, eat and drink a lot.

Chapter Eight

Wednesday night at the quilting club meeting, Maggie and Nan had a lot to talk about. They showed the pictures they had taken and the ones from the internet. Everyone commented and wished that they had been able to go.

Beth asked, "How long did it take you guys to hike into these places?"

"We only had to hike to a couple of sites. Mostly we were able to drive," divulged Nan.

"Bet you were bellyaching on the two you did hike," laughed Beth.

"Maybe," said Maggie and Nan in unison with a smirk. Everyone laughed.

"Ok, enough about us. Has anyone heard anything about the horse poaching while we were gone?" asked Maggie. Everyone shook their heads no. "Some detectives you are," sighed Maggie. Again, everyone laughed.

"Well, we are back, and I, for one, plan on finding out what is going on. I am going to get some of those game cameras tomorrow and take them out to the area or where I think it was located."

The night was fun, and Maggie completed four more blocks, *slow goes the turtle*, she thought...

The next morning, Maggie went to the Sportsman Warehouse, looking for the game cameras. She walked down the aisle, looking at all the different types and decided on a Stealth Cam QS12 Trail Camera. According to the information, "the QS12 will take up to 10MP per triggering and can also record up to fifteen seconds of video to get a great idea of what is in your target area. Each image will display the time, date, and moon phase giving you an idea of the conditions for each image." This sounded exactly what she needed. However, they're not cheap, and Maggie wanted two. Plus, they cost $69.99 each on sale. She wasn't sure how she could explain that to Pete, so she wouldn't. Maggie would use her own money.

Maggie was frugal and always had some money stashed away. When they went out for an evening and if they gambled, she's usually pretty lucky and would rat-hole some of the winnings for unusual things she needed. In this case, game cameras.

When she got home, she called Nan, "Hey, you want to go back to where we released the horses and put up these cameras I bought?"

Quiet on the other end. "Yeah, I guess, but I just don't like being shot at."

"Agree with that, but if we see horses corralled, we will leave. We can take the binoculars and see quite a distance, hopefully, before they spot us," asserted Maggie.

"What are you going to tell Pete?" Asked Nan.

"A little white lie," as Maggie laughed.

So it was planned that they would leave around ten tomorrow; Bill was at work, and Pete had a 4-H meeting in Gardnerville, so the coast was clear.

The next morning, Maggie didn't tell Pete she was going anywhere; in fact, she was on the computer when he left. While going through her e-mail and Facebook, she saw a reply to the picture inquiry she posted a while back, asking if anyone recognized the area. The guy's name was Gus. He messaged Maggie on Facebook, as he was a little familiar with the area. He was up there last week to check it out for the hunting season. Saw a cattle truck and corrals, no people, just the truck. He thought that was odd. However, he told her how to get to that area. He even posted her a map.

Maggie was elated with the info. Now she knew how to get in and out of the area quickly. Then she got to thinking. Maybe those horses weren't wild, but belong to a rancher who uses them to gather up his cattle. Holy crap, what if that was the case? She sat at her computer with her head down and rubbing her temples. *I am sure they were wild. There weren't saddles or gear to ride them. Well, I hope the camera will tell us what is going on.*

At ten, she honks her horn outside of Nan's house, who came out with her arms full and Shep. They hopped in the Jeep. "I brought lunch because I know you forget," she said with a smirk.

'Oh criminy, you are right, slipped my mind completely. Wait until I tell you some news I received today." Maggie proceeded to tell Nan about the Facebook message and her concerns that maybe the horses belong to a rancher.

"Well, I, for one, don't think a rancher would have shot at us, they would have come out yelling," bubbled Nan.

"Good point, I never thought of that," declared Maggie.

"What did Pete say today, when you lied to him?"

"Nothing, because I never told him," Maggie laughed, "what he doesn't know won't hurt him." They both laugh.

"Well, let's hope there is no shooting today." With that, they took off, as they now had a map.

About an hour or so later, they were back to the area where they released the wild horse. Maggie stopped the Jeep about a quarter of a mile away parking by a little knoll. She hooked up the drone and sent it flying by the corrals, which were still there. The drone didn't show any life and no trucks. Driving up closer, Maggie picked out the spot she wanted to place the cameras. It only took her a few minutes to set them in place, one on each side of the corrals.

"Done. Now let's get the heck out of here," signaled Maggie. "We can go back to where we first stopped and watch the area pretty well without being seen."

"Hopefully, they won't be coming by today," Nan laughs nervously.

"I just wonder who they are?" questioned Maggie.

"I don't know, but I bet BLM is involved somehow. Over the last few years, they have really had a hard-on against the wild horse," blurted out Nan.

"Wow. Tell us how you really feel," laughed Maggie.

They sat, letting the dogs run while they ate their lunch on the tailgate of the Jeep. Around two, seeing nothing had changed, they decided to head home.

"I will come back on Monday to see if the cameras picked up anything," described Maggie, "you don't have to come if you don't want to."

"Shep and I want to come. We have come this far, and I don't want to miss the fun of who they may be," chuckled Nan.

"All for one partner, we may go down together, but we are a team. Love ya."

"Love ya too."

Maggie got home before Pete, so he didn't even know she was gone. Dinner was on the table by the time he got home. All was well.

Chapter Nine

Maggie waited until Monday before she snuck out to the area. She waited for Pete to leave. He again went to a meeting, this time in Reno. Maggie didn't call Nan and knew she would catch heck for that. Nevertheless, she wanted to check on the cameras. Maggie parked by the little knoll to observe the corrals. No one around except a few cattle.

Leaving Yazoo in the Jeep, she crept toward the corrals, again, not seeing anyone in her binoculars. She got to the first camera and took the SB stick out, inserting another one. Sneaking over to the other camera, she repeated the process, then skedaddled back to the Jeep. Firing up her computer, she placed the SB stick and downloaded the pictures... Wow, what is this???

The photos showed the horse poachers rounding the wild horses up with a chopper. It looked like a BLM chopper was herding them slowly into the makeshift corrals. Not the typical procedure, when they chase horses with a helicopter. Sometimes they chase them into barb wire fences.

Wow, now she had proof. Saving the pictures to her computer, she places the SB cards under the seat of her Jeep in an empty potato chip bag, who were these people? Was it BLM? Or who?

She started to head out when she saw a vehicle coming up the road, backing the Jeep down into a little ravine behind the knoll, she was thankful her Jeep was dark gray. Taking out her binoculars, she crept up the hill to see who they were. They looked innocent enough, driving a white 4x4 pickup, no writing on the side, She couldn't make out the plate number, but it was a Nevada plate. *Darn, I wish I knew more about trucks...*

Two men got out and walked over to the corrals and looked around, thank goodness, they didn't see the cameras. After a few minutes of looking around, they got back in their truck and continued up the road to the next canyon or whatever was up there. Maggie thought *they're just looking for hunting spots to use their deer tags, or at least that is what she hoped.*

Turning her Jeep, down the road, she took off as fast as she could just in case they turned around. Her palms were sweating. *This was a dumb thing to come out here by myself, no one knows where I am... Stupid, you are so stupid as she pounded the steering wheel.*

When she got home, she took out the potato chip bag, her computer, and Yazoo, running into the house. Who was she going to tell about these pictures? Well, Nan, of course. She couldn't tell Pete as he would be upset with her. After all, he forbade her to go out there alone. *Like she would listen.*

"Nan, you are not going to believe what I found today?" beamed Maggie on the phone. "I have pictures of the people horse poaching."

'What? How?" replied Nan, all upset. "You didn't take me??

"I snuck out this morning to get the film out of the cameras."

"All by yourself? Maggie, are you nuts? You could have been killed."

"Well, I wasn't, so calm down," snarled Maggie.

"Okay. Okay, I'm calmed down, I just worry about you sometimes. Tell me what you saw," requested Nan.

"Nan, I have pictures of the poachers herding the horses into the corrals with a chopper. A BLM chopper no less," exclaimed Maggie, all excited.

"But why would BLM shoot at us the other day?" asked Nan.

"Good question. Maybe its someone who works for the BLM, and they are doing this on the side... Heck, I don't know??" whined Maggie.

"Do I take the pictures to the cop shop? I am not sure what to do?" whispered Maggie.

"Well, you are going to have to face the music and tell Pete," lectured Nan.

"I can't. I just can't. Better yet, I don't want to," stammered Maggie.

"You know you will have to."

"Let's talk about it at the quilting meeting and see what everyone thinks," urged Maggie.

"Okay, but you are putting off the inevitable," sighed Nan.

Maggie made copies of the pictures and hid the SB cards in the bottom of her sock drawer. She wasn't sure why she was acting so paranoid. The hard part was acting like nothing was going on when Pete came home.

"How was your day?" he asked.

"Was great, did some chores, and played on the computer, and was working on the magazine story. How was your day?"

Maggie kept the talk between them at the basic level, hoping he couldn't see through her. Pete looked at her a couple times quizzically and thought, *she is up to something, bet it has to do with those horse poachers...*

Wednesday night finally came around, and Nan picked her up around 6:15. Maggie was trying to act cool, but busting up inside with all this information. She wondered what the group would say and think.

'Hi, I made pictures from the cameras so you could see what is going on out there," informed Maggie.

Nan looked at them, "Wow. That looks like the BLM chopper, alright. I wonder what is going on?"

"Time will tell, as we solve this mystery," chimed Maggie.

About halfway through the club meeting, Maggie couldn't keep the information to herself, plus she had two glasses of wine. "Girls, take a gander at these pictures that came from the game cameras, " as she plopped them on the table.

"Wow. Is that's the BLM chopper?" Beth asked.

"They really are chasing horses into a corral," stated Mary with a funny look on her face.

"What are you going to do?" questioned Betty.

"Good questions. I'm asking you guys what we should do?" queried Maggie. "I am not sure it's BLM as they wouldn't have shot at us, or least I hope not. But we have to find out who they are?" sputtered Maggie.

The gals all looked at each other and said, "We are in, let's find these guys."

"Nan and I have a plan," smiled Maggie as she explained it to them.

The rest of the evening went fast. Maggie was so proud, she got four more blocks finished.

Chapter Ten

Betty Santos worked for a local Insurance Company and belonged to the local Soroptimist Club. She knew a woman who worked at the local BLM office, who was also a Soroptimist. While they were having lunch, Betty sat next to her and started nosing around.

Betty asked, "Susan, where do you guys keep the BLM chopper?"

"We keep it on a helipad out back in the yard. We keep it there to protect it from vandals, as the yard is secure," said Susan, the BLM Office Manager's secretary.

"Do you guys ever rent it out?" inquired Betty.

"Ha-ha. Nope, strictly government property. Only government- certified pilots can fly it. Why? Are you looking for a chopper?" Susan asked with a raised eyebrow.

"A little bit, Jeff was thinking of using one to stake out some deer hunting areas. A lot easier in a chopper instead of 4-wheeling it."

"Good thought. Might try the airport, maybe there is a pilot you could rent with a chopper," responded Susan.

"How many pilots are on the BLM staff? Maybe one of them is looking for a side job?" Asked Betty.

"We have two. Maybe one could be for hire, I don't know."

"Can I have their names if you don't mind."

"Not a problem, One is Sean Green. The other is Hugh Montgomery," divulged Susan.

Betty and Susan talked about their kids and work, but Betty was excited; she had names to give to the group. However, Betty thought, *this was too easy.*

Mary Normandy worked at the Sheriff's Office in Carson. While working at the front desk with detectives, she started reading different reports. She didn't see any cases about the rustling of wild horses, but did see a report on rustled cattle. The complaint was being turned over to Lyon County as the event happened out in the desert by Silver Springs... Interesting. She made a copy of the report.

One of the detectives came in, and they started to talk. "Anything unusual going on in the area, Dale?" asked Mary.

"Just more drugs getting into the area. Not sure how. All the Departments are talking about it. The Sheriff called in Tri-Net to check it out. The opioid, cocaine and heroin epidemic is gripping communities across the United States and causing over a hundred overdoses per day. It's becoming a national health emergency. No one can figure how the drugs are being distributed in the area," stated Detective Dale Daniels.

"Wow. Are the drugs coming from Mexico?" asked Mary as she was quite interested.

"We assume they are, but not sure how they are moving them around in the states. They must be using people to carry them or something they trust. We will figure it out. See ya later." Dale left for his office.

Mary felt bummed, she didn't have anything to tell the girls, maybe the horse poachers also did cattle rustling?

Maggie and Nan researched the computer to see if anyone was buying wild horses. They found a rancher in Colorado, who had purchased one thousand horses already for ten dollars each from BLM. Supposedly he sold them to people to use, not for slaughter, but BLM didn't track the sales. They also found a rancher in Utah and Nevada that bought a large number of horses, again with no paper trail.

"How could BLM let that happen?" asked Nan.

"No one cares about the wild horses. They cost the federal government money to keep," snarled Maggie. "It is always about the money."

Monday, Maggie and Nan decided to go out and check on the cameras again. Pete had an appointment in Reno again, so he would be gone most of the day. The two of them and the dogs left around 8:30 am. Maggie knew the route by heart by now. Pulling up to the knoll, they got out the binocs and the drone. Maggie linked the drone to the computer. She was getting good at this now... *wow, those lessons are paying off.*

The drone flew around, not spotting any activity, no horses in the corral, Maggie brought it down and put it back in the Jeep.

"Nan, please stay here with the dogs while I go change the SB cards. I will take the two-way radio, buzz me if you see or hear anything." And off she went. It took only a few minutes to exchange the two SB cards. Looking around, she notices lots of tire tracks on the ground. It seems like they brought in a big truck, probably a cattle truck... interesting. Maggie ran back to the Jeep.

Putting one of the cards into the computer, they saw wild horses that were corralled, being channeled to a cattle truck by portable stalls. There were at least two men, could have been more, but they didn't show up on the camera.

"Nan, they are shipping the horses somewhere. The cattle truck plates are Nevada. I can make out part of it, 578H. This is interesting."

Sticking in the other SB into the computer, the other camera just showed the same scene, but from a different angle, Maggie still couldn't make out the plate.

"When I get home, I will blow up the image of the men to see if we know who they might be," exclaimed Maggie. "I wonder where the horses went. The one thing I am gathering is they do the poaching on the weekends, which is interesting, that's when most people come up here looking around. However, the BLM yard is closed, so whoever is flying the chopper would have access to it on the weekend." Maggie rubbed her head. "The only reason I can think that they shot at us was to scare us off. If we had caught them with the BLM chopper, we would have thought it was BLM and left them alone. I have to give this some thought."

"You have a point. I just feel sorry for these horses, damn they are gathering them up anyway and selling them, I wonder why are they poaching? When they could buy them for ten dollars ahead," queried Nan.

"Good point. We're going to have to research some more. Wonder what the other gals found?"

Closing everything down, they headed home. It seems they kept getting more questions than answers.

Chapter Eleven

Wednesday night at the quilting club, all the girls were excited as they each had something to say.

Betty says, "Let me start first, two pilots fly the BLM chopper. I have their names, Sean Green and Hugh Montgomery. In fact, this was too easy. They are the only two people that are allowed to fly the chopper, as they don't rent it out. They keep it in the secured BLM yard. This means the only thing that could happen is that someone either steals the chopper or there are BLM employees involved. I hate to think that. Maybe we can follow these two men around for a day or two to see what they're up to."

"Great job, Betty," complimented Maggie.

Maggie asked Mary, "what did you find out?"

Mary replied, "I didn't find out much, I did hear from one of the detectives that drugs are really on the rise here, but other than that, I didn't hear anything about wild horse poaching, only cattle rustling. So it was sort of a dead end. What'd you guys find out?"

"Nan and I went and check the cameras on Monday we saw that the horses had been corralled and then put into a cattle truck, taken somewhere. However, the camera did pick up part of the cattle truck's plate, it was 578H. I'm not sure that's much help. Mary, do you think you can run that little of the plate through the Department of Motor Vehicles(DMV) from the Sheriff's office?"

Mary said, "I don't know, but I can try there's nothing that says I can't do it according to my job descriptions and rules."

"The only thing that doesn't make sense," stammered Maggie, "is why they would poach horses? They could buy the horses from BLM for next to nothing and not risk getting caught horse poaching and using BLM equipment to do it?"

All the girls looked at each other, and all wondered the same thing. "That is a good question," sighed Betty.

"I also believe when they shot at us, it was to scare us. If we had seen the BLM chopper and the trucks, we would've left them alone. Thinking it was a BLM operation, however, finding the horses with no vehicles, made us think poachers. Maybe they were waiting for the truck. Shoot, I don't know, I have more questions than answers." Maggie wrung her hands and shook her head, "This is just an assumption on my part that they want to scare us off. Perhaps, they were mad at us for letting the horses out."

The girls all shook their heads in unison what Maggie said made sense.

"So I guess it boils down to checking these two gentlemen out and watching the BLM yard. Especially on the weekends. That's when they seem to do their horse roundups. At least according to the cameras," claimed Maggie.

"It is funny they do it on the weekend and not during the week. More people are out in the desert then. Especially now, with people looking around for deer hunting sites after their tags were drawn." Nan stammered.

"I don't know whether to involve law enforcement yet or wait until we have more information on what is going on. What do you guys think?" asked Maggie.

Nan responded, "I think we should wait until we have something that's more concrete."

The rest of the gals looked at each other, saying, "We will leave it up to you guys."

Beth did say, "I sort of agree with Nan, let's solve this situation first and then give it to law enforcement."

They spend the rest of the evening quilting, and Maggie completed five blocks with a personal *wahoo* to herself. Only three trillion to go, or at least that is what it felt like. *However, if I'd make some at home, I would get this thing done quicker* as she laughed to herself.

Maggie and Nan discussed doing a stakeout at the BLM office over the weekend. Maggie was trying to figure out how she could do it without Pete finding out. He had 4-H on Saturday and was gone most of the day. He would be home on Sunday, so it was decided that Maggie would stakeout on Saturday, leaving around eight a.m., and Nan would stakeout on Sunday. They would text each other as to what they saw.

Maggie decided on Saturday morning not to take Yazoo, and he sulked, giving her that look, "Mom, you're not taking me. How come?" Maggie explained to Yazoo, "it might be dangerous. You stay home and take care of the house. Be a good boy," giving him love and a treat. He was sort of happy as he chewed the treat, but he still watched her leave with his head hung down.

She also didn't take the drone. Instead, she just took her binoculars. Trying to find a place to park where she could observe the yard and not be observed was the hardest part. She located a little hill that overlooked part of the town and had a good view of the BLM backyard. The chopper was sitting on the helipad. She thought, *this might be a waste of time, but what the heck.*

Maggie didn't have to wait very long, amazingly, only about ten minutes passed when the chopper blades started running. She didn't see anyone, but somebody was warming up the chopper. She must of miss seeing him. Another man came out of the building, dressed in a dark hoodie, which was odd as it wasn't a chilly morning. She watched him jump into the helicopter, and the chopper flew off in the direction of Silver Springs.

Maggie now faces a dilemma, do I follow them? Do I go to the start of the dirt road going to the horse area and wait to see what happens? She decided on that line of action, calling Nan, she said, "are you up to making a trip, they've taken off in the chopper. I'm thinking of waiting on highway 50 to watch for the cattle truck. Maybe several hours, so bring food. Also, can you stop by the house and pick up Yazoo? He was mad at me this morning for leaving him at home."

Nan laughed, saying, "I know who runs your house."

Maggie responded, "the same one that runs yours. The dog. I will meet you at the Red Hut parking lot."

Twenty minutes later, Nan showed up in the parking lot and climbed into Maggie's Jeep with the food and the dogs. Off they went.

They parked by some buildings, so they weren't apparent to anyone coming or going up the dirt road. Nan had brought apple fritters and a thermos of coffee, so they sat eating and drinking coffee. Maggie feared it would be a couple hours or better before anything happened. As the poachers had to round up the horses in a corral and then transfer them into the cattle truck. It could take four hours or more.

Around two p.m., their patience paid off. Of course, their butts were tired from sitting that long. The cattle truck with Nevada license plates 578H came rumbling down the dirt road. Maggie was now able to get the full license plate, it was 578HTC. A lone man was driving the truck and was headed for Fallon. Maggie fired up her Jeep and followed, staying back four car lengths.

When he got to Fallon, he headed toward the Fallon Naval Airbase, which trains for "Top Gun" pilots but kept on going toward Schultz. About five miles outside of Fallon, he turned right on the paved road. Now was the tricky part.

There were no other cars, and she didn't want to be obvious that she was following him, so she speeded up and passed, watching him from the rearview mirror.

The truck drove for about another three miles, then turned left on a dirt road. Maggie pulled over and waited a few minutes, so the cattle truck wouldn't spot them turning around. She headed back up the road and slowed down by the dirt road it had a big sign hanging over the entrance; Desert Rats Ranch.

Taking out her binoculars, she looked around, "Wow Nan, there's a whole bunch of horses out there. What is going on? It's like a horse feedlot. I wonder if they have a slaughterhouse too? However, being in Fallon, if you were slaughtering horses, somebody would notice it."

She passed the binoculars to Nan so she could see. All that Nan could say was, "Wow, there's at least eighty horses out there. What in the heck is going on?"

Maggie said, "There's only one way to find out. Let's go up and ask."

"But it could be dangerous," stated Nan.

"True," commented Maggie as she drove her Jeep up the dirt road toward some buildings and the cattle truck. Maggie unhooked her gun, just in case. She saw three men standing by the cattle truck talking. "Hey, guys," she yelled, "What's going on?"

The men turned around and looked at her with a quizzical look on their faces but didn't respond. Maggie went on further, "I notice you like to gather up wild horses and haul them over here. Why?"

She had her gun under her shirt unseen by the guys, but it didn't give her a lot of confidence. There were three of them. One of the men walked over and said, "I'm Jeff Bloom, and this is Desert Rat Ranch, I'm the owner. It's not what it seems. We rescue wild horses from the slaughterhouses and the drug cartels."

Maggie was perplexed now, "why are you using BLM equipment to gather up these horses to save them when BLM sells them to ranchers who slaughter them."

The man wearing the hoodie spoke, "That's not true BLM doesn't sell the horses to ranchers for slaughter, they sell to ranchers for them to use the horse or find the horse a home."

Maggie said, "I'm not going to argue with you. You have a rancher in Colorado, one in Utah and one in Nevada who buys hundreds of horses and BLM has not followed up on any paperwork proving they all found homes and the horses weren't slaughtered?" The man, who was one of the men from the chopper, stepped back with a hung head and didn't say anything more.

The three men looked at each other and Maggie. Jeff saw the other woman in the Jeep and asked them to come in for a cup of coffee so he could explain the whole story to them.

"It's not what it looks like, we're trying to save the horses mainly from being drug mules."

Maggie looked at him with a quizzical face, "Drug mules?"

"Come on in, and we will explain everything, it's complicated. However, Howard has to get the cattle truck back to the rancher who owns it," commented Jeff.

Howard jumped in the cattle truck, drove over to a field and released the horses, then departed to wherever. Maggie watched him until he left.

Maggie waved Nan to hop out of the Jeep and join her, and they all proceeded into the house. Jeff introduced the other man as Charlie while Maggie and Nan introduced themselves.

Jeff made a fresh pot of coffee, which he put on the table with sugar and cream and added some blueberry muffins. "Make yourself at home and let me explain this story to you." Jeff proceeded to say, "Every weekend for the past six months, we have been trying to capture six to ten wild horses. We then bring them to the Desert Rat Ranch to save them. We only gather the mares and their foals if they have one. The animals are treated quite well here on the ranch, and we do find homes for them. You are right about BLM selling horses to different ranchers and not following up on the paperwork. That has been one of our biggest concerns. We believe that many of the horses are being slaughtered." Jeff went on to say, "I think they may try to find homes for the better horses, but, the older horses are given to the drug cartels. Nobody owns these horses, nobody cares, and after they do their job, they're slaughtered. Cut and dried."

Maggie looked at Jeff, "Why would the drug cartels want the wild horses, they're not packhorses. How are they going to use them to pack drugs to different states?"

No one responded. Then Jeff said, "They plant the cocaine, OxyContin, or heroin in the horse's vagina. They then shipped the horse to different states. No one suspects as they are shipped with sales papers proving that they been bought by the person receiving them. Once the buyer gets the horse, they remove the drugs from the horse's vagina, usually around a hundred thousand dollars worth, by slaughtering the horse."

Nan looked at him with disbelief, "Why would they need to kill the horse? If they packed the horse's vagina with drugs, they could remove them the same way."

Jeff responded, "easier said than done when they packed the drugs into the horse, there are barb's on the package so the horse can't reject the drug packages from their body. The only way to remove the drugs is to kill the horse. Then they sell the horse for dog food or sell it for human consumption or just buried it."

Both Nan and Maggie looked at him in disbelief, "This is a hard story to buy. Do you have proof?"

Jeff answered, "we're working on that as we speak. I am not at liberty to tell you how we will get our proof. But we do know, there is a big operation occurring in the area."

"Fine. Fine. But also, the time we released the horses from the corral," growled Maggie, "someone shot at us. Was that you folks?"

Charlie hung his head and very sheepishly said, "yes mam, it was me, I was trying to scare you off. First, I thought maybe you wanted to steal the horses. Then when you let them go, you wasted a whole day's worth of work by letting them out. I was mad as hell. We were waiting for the cattle truck, which was late.

Maggie looked at him glaringly, "well, you made me angry too. You scared the hell out of us and shot a hole in my spare tire, which cost me a two-hundred and twenty dollars for a new one. You could have killed us!"

"Wouldn't happen, I am an excellent shot. The tire shot was to make sure you didn't come back," replied Charlie.

"Well, it didn't work, did it?" Snapped Maggie.

Jeff said, "how did you find out what we're doing?"

"We didn't know what you were doing, so I put cameras out there to watch and see what was going on. And here we are today," responded Maggie with a smirk.

Jeff asked, "Who else knows about all of this?"

Maggie responded quickly, maybe too fast, "Quite a few as I have shared the SB cards with Lyon County law enforcement, plus pictures of the corrals, etc."

Jeff got up from the table, looked at Maggie very intense, and pace the floor, saying, "Damn, we were trying to keep this a secret to protect these horses, until we had all the proof we needed. I'm not sure who we can trust. We aren't sure who works for the cartels, and that includes law enforcement."

Maggie jumped up now and said, "I trust law enforcement overall, there may be a bad apple now and then, but not in any of the people that we have talked with. I don't know who runs the drug cartels or anything about them. But I'm sure the officers in Tri-Net do and will do whatever is possible to slow them down."

Jeff just looked at her, searching her face and said, "I hope what you say is true. Now, what are you going to do with what you have learned?"

"I'm going to research and find out what you say is true, and if so, we will get to the bottom of this. We may not be able to stop it, but we might be able to put a big hole in the operation. And at this point, we will not say anything about the horses that you are protecting on your ranch and pray you are telling the truth." Maggie and Nan proceeded to leave. "We will keep you in the loop of what we find out. We will probably be back."

Jeff responded, "Thank you for helping us. Be safe as you are now in danger from the drug dealers. We will also stay in contact with you."

"Why do you say we are in danger?" inquired Nan.

"They have been watching this ranch and us, trying to figure out how to get to the horses," sighed Charlie.

Maggie stammered, "Darn. I guess if we could find you, so could they. I don't like this at all."

"Neither do we, but we will do anything to protect the horses," surmised Jeff.

Maggie and Nan got into the Jeep as quickly as they could, turning it around and leaving the ranch. Maggie said to Nan, "I've never been so scared in all my life."

Nan commented, "you didn't act it, but I was too. "It's a good thing we are both excellent bullshitters."

They both laughed in unison, knowing they would have to watch their backs. If what Jeff said was right, they could be in for some serious stuff.

Chapter Twelve

Maggie spent the morning researching drug mules on the internet. She always thought they were just people who carried drugs in various places in their body. She read the following:

"Popularly known as 'drug mules,' the victims are made to swallow balloons containing illicit drugs and are then transported across borders. Once they have reached their destination, these balloons are retrieved from the victim's body. The balloons are made with multilayered condoms and are often force-fed to the victim."

She went on to read about an international drug trafficking ring that forced dogs to swallow bags of cocaine and then brutally sliced the animals open to retrieve them. Maggie almost barfed reading about that. They even use puppies. She further read about a Veterinarian who was arrested for using eight-week-old puppies as mules to transport something illegal. Then they were killed. It's a horrific case of animal abuse.

Maggie was sickened by what she read. She even found an article by a drug dealer, bragging by damn on the internet, "According to the cartel leader, Jesus Cabureno, the cartel is currently weighing all of the pros and cons of using horses as drug mules. A horse is a pretty standard way of drugs being smuggled. Drugs can be hidden in the uterus' of the horses.

"There are lots of things to take into account when deciding who to use as a drug mule," Cabureno testified. "We want to avoid suspicion as much as possible, so a horse is definitely good for that. They also have extremely big stomachs and anal cavities so we could cram enough coke inside him to fund an entire Donald Trump Presidential campaign."

Maggie then found the story of Cabureno's involvement with the puppies. This man had to be sick! "As alleged in the indictment, Cabureno is not only a drug trafficker, but he also betrayed the veterinarian who pledged to prevent animal suffering when he used his surgical skills in a cruel scheme to smuggle heroin in the abdomens of puppies," U.S. Attorney said shortly after the extradition. "Dogs are mans' best friend, and, as this defendant is about to learn, we are drug dealers' worst enemy."

Maggie couldn't believe what she was reading. Horses and dogs were war heroes in World War I, hauling the wounded. They were also used in World War II and Vietnam. Even today, they are helping our troop scout for explosives, search and rescue, and communications. They are heroes... not drug mules.

Now they are being used as throwaway animals. What kind of world do we live in? Is getting high worth killing animals? *Heck, yes, it's all about the money.* Maggie sat at her desk and cried, thinking about the atrocities that are being done to these animals.

Wednesday night at the quilting club meeting, Maggie was very solemn. Beth asked, "Did you learn anything new about the horse poachers?"

"We did, but at this time, we can't discuss it." as Maggie looked over to Nan. Nan shook her head in agreement.

"What gives?" asked Betty, "I thought you were all gung-ho to solve this mystery."

"We are. We're working on it. However, it has come to light; there could be some danger involved. We don't want you ladies getting hurt," squeaked Maggie.

Everyone looked at them with quizzical faces. "Sorry," said Nan.

"Well, I for one want to be involved," said Betty. "Me too," chimed Beth. Mary never said a word, just looked at them all. Finally, she said, "We are in this together, come hell or high water. "Everyone was in shock, Mary had cussed.

A burst of nervous laughter arose, then the clicking of wine glasses and the pack was understood. All for one. Maggie and Nan then when on to tell the girls what they had found out. Everyone was in disbelief.

"They actually kill the animals," cried Betty. "Innocent puppies? May they rot in purgatory."

"Them are harsh words, Little Lady," snicker Nan, using a John Wayne accent. Betty just looked at her like she was nuts.

"Now, for the worst part, we could all be in danger by getting involved in this situation. According to Jeff, these guys don't mess around. He said they have been watching his place. Personally, I think, if we found them so easily, so could the cartel, So I am inclined to believe him," theorized Maggie.

"What do we do next?" asked Beth.

"I am not sure. Nan and I now think these folks at the Desert Rat Ranch are poaching the horses to save them.

However, I am going to go back out and check on the cameras tomorrow and see if any other activity has occurred. Anyone want to come along?" Maggie explained.

Like always, everyone was busy except Nan. So they planned on a morning trip. The rest of the evening went fast. Maggie finished another block. Around nine, the group broke up and started going to their cars.

They didn't notice the white pickup in the lot across the street from the store. It had two men watching the group activities as they all left Fabric Chicks. When Nan and Maggie left, the pickup followed. Maggie didn't pay any attention until they got to Jack's Valley turnoff.

"Nan, I think we are being followed by a pickup behind us. I am going to wander around just to be sure," stated Maggie calmly.

She turned onto Mica drive, then took a left, then a right, sure enough, about hundred yards back was a white pickup truck. Maggie speeded up and pulled into a cul-de-sac and pulled into a driveway, turning off her lights. The pickup went by. They sat there for a few minutes, not saying a word, then Maggie drove over to the Target parking lot and parked among the workers' cars. There they could watch Jack's Valley road. Neither of them said a word, as both were scared to death. After a few minutes, they saw the white pickup, go to the light, and turn toward Carson City.

"Wow, now I can breathe," chimed Nan with a sigh of relief.

"Me too, I almost peed my pants. I wonder who they were?" Asked Maggie as she started up the car to take Nan home. "I am going to have a drink of wine when I get home? She said laughingly.

Nan laughed and said, "me too."

Chapter Thirteen

Thursday morning, after Pete left the house to go to the Doctors, Maggie and Yazoo snuck out of the house and picked up Nan.

"This shouldn't take but an hour or so, just going to remove the cameras," stated Maggie.

Maggie did like she always has, and parked behind the little knoll, got out the drone and flew it over the area. No sign of life, even the corrals were gone. Seeing they found out about Jeff, she guesses he moved their operation to a different spot.

Maggie ran and disconnected the two cameras, then hustled back to the Jeep. These darn things cost too much to lose. Firing up the computer, she placed one of the cards to see what had happened since they were here last.

"Nan, look at this. The only thing that shows up is a white king cab pickup with two guys. The other day when I was here, that same truck with two men showed up. I didn't think much about them figuring they were looking for a hunting site for the deer draw. But now I wonder, especially after last night, as that was a white pickup."

"Let's get out of here, just case they are watching this area with binoculars."

"Good idea." Maggie fired up the Jeep and headed down the road. She looked in her rearview mirror to see if they were being followed, but nothing.

"Do you think we should go to the cop station with what we have?" asked Nan.

"What do we have? The only thing we have is the horse poachers, and we don't want to give them up," replied Maggie.

"True, I just think maybe we are getting in over our heads in this mess," commented Nan.

"Nah. I have some good pictures of these guys, lets nose around and see if anyone knows them. If they look like bad guys, we will turn them over to the cops. When I get home, I will print the pictures out."

"Okay, for now. Let's give that a try. But I want to tell you I am scared," whimpered Nan.

"Me too," sighed Maggie.

When Maggie got home, she went into the office and printed the pictures of the guys. The camera got some good shots, both times. They were the same guys she saw the time when she was out there. Was that a coincidence?

"Hi, Hon, I am home," and Pete came walking into the office.

Maggie jumped up to cover the pictures, giving Pete a hug, "how did things go?"

"Fine. What are you doing with pictures of a couple of my 4-H fathers? Pete reached around her to pick up the photos.

'You know these guys?" asked Maggie with a quizzical look on her face.

"Yep, Randy and Robert Wilson, twin brothers. I have their boys, Matt, and Mark in archery." Pete looked at Maggie and said, "Okay, what have you been up to?"

All Maggie could say was, "Wow. You know who they are, that is interesting."

"Maggie, spill!"

Maggie looked at Pete, and she knew she couldn't lie. "I think these guys have something to do with drugs and wild horses."

Pete looked at her, astonished, "They are in the construction business together and good fathers, their boys are excellent archers or bowman. According to the fathers, the whole family bow hunts. I understand they are all experts in archery, better known as a toxophilite. Why do you suspect them being involved in drugs?"

Maggie hung her head, "I don't have proof yet, but I'm working on it. Let me bring you up to date." She then proceeded to tell Pete what she had been doing and what she had found out about the horse poachers, the Desert Rat Ranch, and the cartel using horses as drug mules. "These guys keep popping up on the camera at the corral area."

Pete just looked at her, "Even after I told you not to get involved. I told you it could be dangerous, but oh no, you think you are Nancy Drew." Pete paced the office, clearly upset.

"Okay, I get it; you are angry at me. You will even be madder when I tell you what I plan to do now. Nan and I are going to follow these guys, that you so kindly identified and see what they are really up to. Maybe they are innocent, perhaps they are not.

"Like horse pucky, you are unless I am involved. Period! End of discussion," as he stormed off.

Maggie sat in the office, looking at the photos, listening to her husband slamming things in the kitchen. She thought, *why are men so bullheaded.*

For the next two days, she and Nan followed the white Chevy King cab pickup. It apparently belongs to Robert Wilson. They watched his house as he left for work, picking up his brother and ending at their construction site. They did nothing out of the ordinary. In fact, it was boring. Maggie thought *I could never be a cop on a stakeout.*

Maggie stayed in touch with Pete by phone. She texts him as they were hardly speaking to each other. "Sitting down the road from 2356 Curry St, the construction site of the Wilson Bros. So far, nothing unusual."

"You won't find them doing anything wrong. They are good people. It's a waste of your time," replied Pete.

After six hours, Maggie gave up and went home. *I hate stakeouts...*

Saturday morning, Maggie went to archery with Pete to meet the gentlemen in question.

Pete introduces Maggie to the children and their parents. She said, "Hi. I am here to track your scores for the State Tournament in Las Vegas, to see if you are eligible to participate. So don't mind me," she laughed as she pulled out a binder. "How many of you plan on going? " About ten hands out of the fifteen children raised their hands. "Awesome, and we are going to bring all the medals home." The kids and parents laughed.

Maggie did her paperwork and watched the Wilson fathers and noticed nothing out of the ordinary. After about an hour, she moved over by them as they were standing together. "Your boys are excellent at archery."

"Yeah, they have been shooting since they were seven. Now that they are eleven, they can qualify for Junior Olympics," disclosed Randy.

"Wow. You must be proud of them," affirmed Maggie.

Both men beamed like proud peacocks. Maggie thought, *maybe they aren't drug dealers, but why do they always show up. But she was still curious.*

"Are you guys going deer hunting with your bows this year?" asked Maggie.

"Yep, we go every year. We have already been checking out spots to see which areas are best for the draw. Looks like around the Stagecoach area," declared Robert. After a second or two, Robert said, "I just remembered, we

113

heard you were shot at somewhere in the Virginia Range after you had released some horses. The funny part is Randy, and I saw portable corrals in that area a couple of times when we were up there, and just figured it was BLM. Glad no one shot at us."

Maggie sighed, "Yes, we never found out who shot at us. However, we turned everything over to the Lyon County Sheriff's Department."

Well, glad you are okay, that had to have been scary," smiled Robert. Maggie thought, *well guess it is not these guys... darn, this isn't going to be easy.*

When Maggie got home, she called Nan and told her it was unsuccessful, they didn't look like the dealers. Pete came in and gave her one of his looks. "Told you they weren't dealing in drugs. They are super guys."

"If it walks like a duck and quacks like a duck, it's usually a duck," sneered Maggie. " I have pictures of their truck."

"Whatever, there is no talking to you," as Pete walked out of the kitchen.

Maggie wanted to scream at him as he left. *Can't you sit down and discuss this matter. I am interested in your thoughts.* But instead, she said nothing, just fumed.

Getting up and going to the office helped her relax. She turned on her computer and again reviewed the tapes. She even looked at what the drone had filmed. After about an hour, she noticed something on the drone videotape from the day they were shot at. She increased the size, and there in the distance was a white pickup, king cab, just like the Wilsons. It was hidden behind some tall sagebrush in the back of the portable corrals. It's possible that the poachers didn't know it was there.

"Pete, can you come here for a moment?"

"Yeah. What do you need?"

"Look at this picture. What do you see?" asked Maggie.

"A white king cab pickup. It looks like it might be a late model dodge. Why?

"The drone picked this up on the day we were shot at. Is that the Wilson truck?"

"No, they have a Chevy, king cab."

Maggie looked disappointed, "They all look alike."

"Not even, they are just both white," laughed Pete.

"Criminy, I wish I knew more about vehicles."

"So what you are looking for is a Dodge King cab probably about 2012, maybe 2013. There are a couple dozen around here. They are a pretty popular work truck," commented Pete.

"Yeah, and it could come from anywhere," sighed Maggie with a long face. The bad part is I don't know how to find it."

"Can you blow up the picture anymore to get a partial plate?"

"No. Any more, and it will distort the picture."

"Well, at least you now know it is not the Wilson Brothers."

"True. I knew that was too easy."

Chapter Fourteen

Wednesday night, Maggie told the girls what she had found out "Nothing. It looks like we are back to the drawing board. The only thing we have going for us is we are looking for 2012/2013 white Dodge King Cab pickup."

Everyone shook their heads. They didn't know anyone who owned the white pickup. Mary said, 'It looks like we have hit a dead end."

"Yeah, sort of" conceded Nan.

"Aw, come on, we can't give up now, Mary, can you search DMV for this area for white pickup?" Asked Beth.

"I can try, but don't think I will be too successful."

The conversation of the evening went on and with everyone a little down. But after a few glasses of wine and Maggie finishing another block, the group got enthused.

I am going back to the Desert Rat Ranch and see if they have any leads, who wants to come?" Like always, everyone was busy except Nan, so the two of them would go tomorrow.

Thursday morning, the four of them, plus the dogs, took the ride to Fallon. Pete had talked Bill into coming too. Pete said he wanted to keep the girls safe, but really he wanted to meet these supposed horse poachers. Bill was also curious. They were so busy talking they didn't notice the white Dodge pickup several cars back tailing them.

Jeff came out to meet them when they drove into his ranch. "Hi. I see you brought company."

"Yes, we brought our husbands." Whom Maggie introduced to Jeff. "They think we might be in danger," Maggie laughed.

"Well, someone has been trying to steal the horses, we have hired a few extra hands to protect them. They even took a pot shot at us," stated Jeff.

"Did you call the authorities?" asked Bill.

"No, for obvious reasons," Jeff smirked, "these wild horses have been poached." Jeff went on to tell the men, he thought the cartel was behind the shootings and why. Maggie was glad they heard the story from Jeff. She felt that just maybe Pete didn't believe her... *imagine that?* Maggie proceeded to tell Jeff about the white Dodge king cab pickup and how they were trying to find out who it belongs to.

"Good luck with that, it will be like finding a needle in the haystack. Most ranchers drive a white king cab or extended cab pickup in these parts," replied Jeff.

"Yeah, we know, but we are working on it. Have you gathered up any more horses?" inquired Pete.

"Maybe ten, brought them in from the Virginia Range. But after the shooting incident, we have been laying low, " stated Jeff. "Did find homes for eight horses, so it has been a good week."

Jeff invited them into the house for something to drink, but everyone said no, they were going to head out. Maggie said, "We just came by to educate our husbands and see if anything new had happened," Maggie gave Jeff her cell number, and he gave her his.

Maggie said, " If we learn anything, I will let you know."

Jeff said the same thing. After a few more minutes of talking, they got back into the Jeep and started the drive back home.

The white pickup was watching them with binoculars. They watched the Jeep Wrangler leave an head back toward Carson City. They also headed back in that direction. Traffic, this time of the day, was light going to Carson. Bruno and Macks decide that maybe they would try to run them off the road, mainly as a warning. The boss wanted them to scare them off; however, Bruno didn't want to damage the boss's truck. Best of all, it did have cattle bars in the front. Outside of Fallon, going up a hill, they saw an opportunity. The men didn't want to kill them, just scare them, so this was a safe bet.

Pete said very calmly, "I don't want to alarm you, but tighten your safety belts, we have a white Dodge pickup coming up fast. I believe they are going to try and ram us."

Maggie quickly looked around and saw the upcoming pickup, fear crossed her face as they got closer, but the best part she got a look at the Nevada plate. "784Y, phooey, they have mud or something smeared on the rest. There's two men inside," she muttered.

Pete said, "I'm going to go off the road, just about the time they think they are going to hit us. So hang on."

The truck was about three feet from the Jeep when Pete swerved and drove off the road on the right, hitting the dirt, while stomping on the gas and slamming the brakes all at the same time. It made the Jeep spin and slide up the side of the mountain. The big pickup couldn't swerve fast enough to follow and went barreling by without hitting them.

Pete finally got the Jeep stopped and took a deep breath. "Everyone okay?"

Nervous laughter broke out. "Wow," said Bill, "are they coming back?"

"Nope, I bet they are long gone, of course, they could be laying in wait, but my gut is telling me probably not," concluded Pete. He opened the door and walk around, all looked okay, few scratches, but nothing serious. Hopping back in, he heard the girls say, in unison, "Now do you believe us."

The men in the white pickup were not happy as they headed to Carson to talk to the boss. "We got to scare off these nosy people somehow. Between them and the people in Fallon, they are cramping our operation. I hope the boss has some ideas," lamented Macks.

On getting home, Maggie called Mary, "Mary, I have a partial license plate number on that 2012/2013 white Dodge King cab diesel pickup. You think you can run it and get some information?"

"I will try what is it?" She said hesitantly.

"784Y, a Nevada plate, looks like one of the newer ones."

"Well, I go to work tomorrow, will run, and see if we can bust these bad guys. How did you get it?"

Maggie told her what had happened that morning. "I can't believe how brazen they were to try and run us off the roads. Thank goodness, Pete was driving. Thanks for your help, and hopefully you will have something by Wednesday night or sooner."

"I let you know as soon as I have something. Talk to you later."

Chapter Fifteen

Friday morning at the Sheriff's Office, Mary ran the partial plate. Boy, this is like finding a needle in a haystack. 784Y was a high plate number, knowing it belongs to a white Dodge diesel pickup helped, but the overall plate run was about three hundred vehicles long. Mary started going through the list to find Dodge pickups. After about an hour, she found three 784Y plates belonging to Dodge pickups. One was 2012 784YDL belonging to a Rita Jones in Minden, two were 2013 784YFH, belonging to Sam Brown of Dayton and 784YKZ, belonging to Ace Sorenson of Six Mile Canyon, in the Dayton area.

Well, that's a start, she had the full addresses, now they could stake these folks out to see which one was the bad guy.

Mary gave Maggie a call and passed on the information. "Thank you so much, Mary. Tomorrow we will start watching these folks."

Maggie called Nan to give her the news. "Tomorrow, we will start the stakeouts... ha-ha."

"Is Pete going to let you do it, or is he helping?" inquired Nan.

"He is like my shadow. So you guess?"

Maggie then called Jeff and gave him the information. "Watch for those license plates. If you see a white Dodge pickup, check the plates."

"Thanks, Maggie. Will do," he said a little hesitantly.

Saturday was a busy day for the McDonald family. They have a hot rod, and today was a car show at Fuji Park in Carson City. The McDonalds have a 1968 Chevy Chevelle SS, orange and Nan, and Bill have 1956 Chevy Belair, blue and white. This show leads up to Hot August Nights in just a few weeks.

Maggie was frustrated as she couldn't go playing Nancy Drew until Monday. Showing the car was a family project. She called Betty to see if she could watch the pickup in Minden. "Betty, I would really appreciate it if you could just watch Rita Jones. Don't connect with her, as it could be too dangerous if she is the bad guy. If you can get a description of her and so forth."

"Yes, I can watch for about four hours, but that is all I can spare, as I pick up the grandkids late this afternoon. Will that help?"

"Will have to do. Thanks for your help," sighed Maggie *thinking I can't ask Beth as she has a store to run. Plus, Mary has done enough already.*

Maybe after the car show, I could snoop around. Pete and I could drive by the two in the Dayton area. Maggie thought *I wanted to look at the truck to get a feel.*

That night after the show, Pete begrudgingly agreed to go check out the trucks. "What do you hope to find Maggie? A sign that says, bad guys?"

"No. But maybe we will get a feel. You saw the truck that tried to run us off the road," chirped Maggie

"Okay, you have a point," conceded Pete.

The first place they drove to was the Dayton address. The white king cab Dodge diesel pickup was sitting in the driveway of a tract home, no cattle guards. The house looks like it had little kids, as toys were in the yard. Both Pete and Maggie ruled this off the list. Maggie thought *this is too easy, we are missing something.*

Pete drove up to the six-mile canyon address, this was the residence of the second pickup. There was an older home on what looked like five acres, sort of run-down, the truck was not home. *Darn.* We will have to come back. They didn't see any life around the property except for two big older black labs in the yard. Maggie didn't want to get out as the dogs didn't look all that friendly. This stop will be for another day. Maggie wondered what Betty found out and gave her a call.

"Hey, Betty, how did it go today?" Maggie could hear children in the background. Betty yelled at the kids to turn the TV down. "Nothing exciting. I found the address and watch the vehicle like we talked about."

"Did the truck have cattle bars on the front?" Maggie asked.

A pause for a second, "Yes. Yes, it did. It looked like it might be a ranch truck, had some dents."

"Did you see a driver?"

"No. I saw an older woman and a man, but they were just in the yard, doing some yard work. Like I said, nothing exciting."

"Well, we are whittling them down, out of the three pickups, one for sure has a guard. So you're checking on that truck was a big help. Thank you so much." About then, Maggie heard a crash. "Have to go, one of the kids just broke something," and Betty hung up.

Maggie told Pete what she learned from Betty.

Sunday, Pete and Maggie drove out to six-mile canyon again to check on the truck. No truck was in the driveway this time either or on the property. They went to Minden to check on the other vehicle and have dinner at Sharkey's Casino.

Rita Jones's place was a charming ranch style home with what looked like five acres. The truck was also not home. Maggie did notice four horses on the property, one was most definitely a Mustang, which usually means it was adopted from BLM or the Northern Nevada Correctional Center. *Interesting.*

After dinner, they again drove by the Jone's place, but no truck. They headed home to feed Yazoo.

Monday morning, Maggie and Nan met at the Red Hut for breakfast and to discuss their plans. "I feel like we are spinning our wheels," commented Maggie, not a patient person. "Nothing is happening."

"I disagree," said Nan, "we broke it down to a possibility of two trucks, and solved the horse poaching situation. Not bad if you asked me."

"But who is behind all the crap?" snapped Maggie.

"You're an author, use your whiteboard, like you're writing a story," suggested Nan.

"Good point, now I know why we are like blood sisters," Maggie laughed, "I never thought to use the whiteboards. When I get home, that is exactly what I am going to do?" Maggie paused for a second, "You want to go to six-mile canyon with me, I think the clues are there,"

"Sure, what the heck," whispered Nan.

Neither woman noticed the two people in a booth behind them, listening intently to their conversation. The two got up and paid their bill and left. A few minutes later, Maggie and Nan got up to go.

Chapter Sixteen

They drove to the address on Six Mile Canyon road, and this time the white Dodge diesel pickup was home. It had cattle guards, some dents in the body. It looked like a ranch truck. Maggie stated, "I just have a feeling about this one, not sure, no proof."

"Well, we can watch it from afar, we have the binoculars. Because I am not going in there... period. So don't even try to talk me into it."

Maggie gave Nan a begging dog look.

"Nope, not even, if these people kill puppies and horses, what stops them from killing me?" divulged Nan.

"Damn, do you always have to be so logical. You are right, we need to come prepared."

Nan snapped, "You come prepared," and they both looked at each other and laughed.

Driving up the road, they found a side street that gave them a decent view of the truck and parked behind some scrub pines. After several hours, nothing happened, no people and the truck just sat there. *Darn, I hate stakeouts... so dull, thought Maggie. Well, at least we know two of the vehicles have cattle guards, and I am placing my money on this one.* Around four, they decided to head home.

After dinner, Maggie retired into the office. She had some writing to do. The short story about the airmail arrows was coming due to the magazine. Even with everything going on, she still had a job.

A couple of hours later, she had completed her story and sent it off to the beta readers. Maggie had three people who read her materials and critiqued for errors. They should have the story back to her in the next day or so. Then she would do the rewrites before sending it to the editor.

The evening was early. Going into the kitchen for a glass of wine. Maggie retrieved the whiteboard and started mapping out what had been happening with the horse poachers at the kitchen table.

1. The drone, learning how to use it.
2. The airmail arrows. Looking for some in the Virginia Range.
3. Finding the horse poachers the first time and getting shot at.
4. Buying and setting up deer cameras.

5. Catching BLM choppers rounding up the horses.

6. Following the chopper to the cattle truck to the poachers.

7. The 2012/13 white dodge diesel king cab pickup running them off the road.

8. Finding three Dodge diesel pickups and now deciding who's the bad guys.

Something is missing... what? Maggie rubbed her chin and thought. After fifteen minutes or so, she said to herself. *What happened to the pilot of the BLM chopper. Which one? Sean Green or Hugh Montgomery? The bad guys also have to have a ranch to place the horses they bought from BLM. Maybe looking for the Dodge pickup is the tail of the dog, and we need to find the head.* She sat rubbing her forehead, trying to see what plan of action to take next.

9. Find the BLM pilot.

10. See if Betty can find out to whom BLM sold the horses in this area.

Yazoo came up to her, whining like he wanted to go out."Okay, boy, let me get my slippers." Maggie leaned down to put her slippers on, as a bullet came whizzing through the window by her left shoulder, she quickly fell to the floor. Pete came running into the room, turning off the lights. At the same time, he heard a diesel truck out in front take off. "You okay, Maggie?"

"Yes. Scared, but okay, it could have killed me."

Yazoo thought this was great, as he was licking her face. Maggie was afraid to get up, she was shaking and about ready to throw up from fear and clung to the dog.

Pete was on the phone calling 911, "We just had a shooting at our house. 4206 Greenwood Lane, Jacks Valley. Send an officer." Pete sounded calm, but Maggie knew he was scared and upset.

The Sheriff deputies arrived in no time, two cars. The bullet had come through the kitchen window, went straight through the open french doors by the dining room, into the library, and into a book. They pried out the bullet, "it looks like a .223," the officer said.

They figured it was a high powered rifle, as the velocity of the bullet didn't shatter the kitchen window. They were fortunate there wasn't more damage done to the house.

Maggie was really shaken because of all the "what if's" that had taken over in her mind. Pete was pacing, and he was angry. Maggie was also. How dare someone violate her in her own home. She had to solve this problem quickly before someone got hurt. She didn't like being shot at, especially in her own home. This was twice now she had been shot at.

The police took their report and the bullet, they took lots of pictures, said they would put extra patrols in the neighborhood. There was little more they could do and left. Maggie and Pete knew they were right, but it didn't make them feel any better.

Maggie thought *I won't be sitting by a window at night anymore.* As she pours herself another glass of wine, Pete had already gotten a beer. She promptly called Nan and told her what had happened and warn her to be careful, just in case. *Who are these people?* Thought Maggie

The next morning, Maggie called Betty to see if she could get a list of the buyers from BLM. "I will try, but I'm not sure if that is private information," chimed Betty.

"I don't see why it would be. Let's say I wanted to buy one of the horses, I would need to know who is selling them."

'True. I will see what I can find out. Let me see, it is Tuesday. I do have a Soroptimist lunch today, so maybe Susan will tell me," commented Betty.

"Also, see if Susan might have an idea which pilot would fly the chopper on the weekend. Good luck, and let me know what you find out," answered Maggie.

"Will do. I am beginning to feel like a real detective," as Betty laughed.

"If you find out the information, you will be a top-notch one in my book," and they both laughed.

Chapter Nineteen

Maggie was glad it was coming up on Hot August Night's, as it would keep Pete's mind off what was happening at home. Things had been quiet, no more problems or shootings. So, Pete was all excited, since it was Hot August Nights week and all. He had been cleaning and polishing the car for two days now. Today was sign-ups in Reno at the Grand Sierra Resort, so off they went. They took their regular vehicle today, as they would be there for several hours. This year's event was planned to have six thousand hot rods.

Maggie and Nan decided to gamble while Pete and Bill retrieved their registration package. The casino was packed. Hot August Nights harken back to the time when hot rods ruled the roads, and custom cars were a way of life. For the McDonalds and the Morgans, it brought back memories of their lives when they were younger, and times were different.

Both Pete and Bill were in Vietnam. Bill in the Navy and Pete in the Air Force. But even with the war, life wasn't as complicated as today.

This six-day vintage car show features cruising parades, exciting drag races, show-n-shine displays. They loved to cruise the Casinos and participate in the poker run. There were musical performances from legendary acts from the 1950s, '60s, and '70s. Maggie thought, *everyone should visit Hot August Nights, even if they don't have a car.*

Tomorrow night they would cruise Sparks and settle in at the Atlantis Casino to hear the music. Both Nan and Maggie would miss their quilt club meeting this week.

Early the next morning, Betty called, "I have the info you wanted on who has bought horses."

"Wow. That's awesome. Do you want to meet for breakfast?"

"Sure, if you are buying?"

"Yep, see you in twenty minutes at Red Hut."

Maggie yelled at Pete, "I am going to meet Betty at Red Hut for breakfast, want to come?"

He came out of the bathroom, drying his hands, "Yeah, that sounds good."

The three of them found a booth, and Betty gave Maggie the list of people that had bought horses, supposedly to sell or use them themselves. It was four pages long. Betty said, "This is only in the last quarter. Also, Susan thinks it is Hugh Montgomery, who flies the chopper on the weekend. He is very sympathetic toward the horses."

"Interesting. I'll have to ask Jeff about him.

Betty also noted that Susan thinks a ranch in Yerington is selling the horses for slaughter.

"Does she have any proof?"

"No. And the funny thing is the new BLM Manager won't let her follow up with them to get proof of who is buying the horses from the seller."

"What is the manager's name?" asked Pete.

"Richard Garcia, he was transferred here from southern California about a year ago. Susan says his family is still in California. The funny part is every weekend he flies home. Apparently, he owns his own plane".

"That has to be expensive, wonder how he does it on a manager's salary?" snorted Maggie.

"I thought the same thing," chimed Betty. "According to Susan, he is not very friendly and doesn't give a damn about the wild horses."

"Interesting. I will have to research him. Thanks, Betty, for all the info, you are a great detective", and they all laughed.

With it being Hot August Night week, Maggie and Nan couldn't do much detective work. Maggie did call Jeff and tell him what little she knew. He told her someone had tried to tear down a fence and steal some of the horses but was not successful. Maggie thought *these guys don't give up. We have to find out who they are?*

Chapter Eighteen

Finally, things calm down, the hot rod was parked in the garage, and Maggie had time to research Mr. Garcia. Supposedly he was a widower with three grown children. Maggie thought *it doesn't make sense to fly to southern Calif every weekend, maybe he has a girlfriend? Darn, keep finding more questions than answer.*

Wednesday night at the quilting club, they all talked about what they had found out. Maggie wrote it all down, so she wouldn't forget. That night she didn't finish her blocks. It seems like they were spinning their wheels.

Maggie stated, "Tomorrow, I'm going to watch Ace Sorenson's house, in Six Mile Canyon. Anyone want to come with me?"

No one volunteered, as stakeouts were boring. "Okay, I will do it myself," as Maggie stuck her tongue out at them. They all laughed.

The next morning Maggie and Yazoo went on the boring stakeout. She had brought food, water, and treats. The truck was parked in front of the house, and where she sat, she had a good view with the binocs. Nine AM came and went, then ten, eleven. Maggie was having a hard time staying awake. Finally, around noon, an older man came out of the house with a cane, he hobbled to the truck, and he had one heck of time getting in, as it was so high; finally, he drove off. Maggie followed about three car lengths behind him.

He drove into Carson City to the Nugget. He parked his truck in a handicap spot and hobbled into the Casino. *Wow, this was a nothing trip, thought Maggie.* But as

Maggie was sitting there, she noticed someone else go into the Casino. *That is odd. I think I will go into the Casino and see what I can see.*

Maggie knew some of the cocktail waitresses that work there. She saw that Penny was working and walked over to her, the casino was not busy.

"Hi Penny, how are you doing?" Questioned Maggie.

"Hey Maggie, doing great, how is Pete?" Replied Penny.

"Mean and ornery as ever. Can you do me a favor?" Asked Maggie.

"Sure. What you need?" Answered Penny.

Maggie went on to explain that a man with a cane came in and could Penny see who he was visiting with if anyone.

"You know I saw him come in and go into the coffee shop. Give me a minute to check."

"Thanks, I appreciate it."

Maggie put a five-dollar bill in one of the penny machines and won seven additional dollars. A few minutes later, Penny came back, "He is sitting with an older woman, and they look like they are having lunch together."

"Could you describe the woman?" Penny described the person that Maggie knew. "Thanks, I really appreciate," drawing out her money, she gave it to Penny as a tip.

Penny said, "You don't have to tip, but thank you." Maggie just smiled and headed out the door. Thinking, *this is an interesting turn of events.*

Maggie stewed all the way home. *How did this person know this man? How could she get that answer?* Maggie called Nan, who answered the phone. "What are you doing right now?"

"I have about three loads of wash that I am doing, why?"

"Do you mind if I come over?" Asked Maggie.

"When did you have to ask? I put some coffee on, and you can help fold," stuttered Nan curious as heck.

"We might need something stronger than that, I have something to tell you. I will be there in ten minutes," said Maggie excitedly.

"I was staking out the guy in six-mile canyon, it is an old man that walks with a cane that drives that white diesel truck. So just for curiosity's sake, I followed him the Carson Nugget Casino and guess who he met??" squealed Maggie.

"Who for Pete's sake?...who?" queried Nan.

Maggie when on to tell her, "I am not sure what to do if anything. It may be an innocent friendship. We don't have any proof that his truck was used to try and run us off the road. If it was his truck, it sure wasn't him driving. As they were two younger men in that truck."

"What you need to do is use your whiteboard and draft this all out, like you are writing a story. Let's see what falls out," urged Nan.

"Good point, you are always so calm and logical," whined Maggie. "Maybe we should talk to Jeff to see if anything new has happened," pointed out Nan.

"Sounds good. Let's take a run-out there see what Jeff thinks," replied Maggie.

"I call Pete and see if he wants to go?" Maggie called the house, no answer, then she called his cell, went into voice mail, so she told him what they were going to do.

Maggie, Nan, Yazoo, and Shep jumped in the Jeep as they drove off to Fallon.

Chapter Nineteen

On the trip over to Fallon, they talked everything out. The whole thing is weird.

"A BLM pilot on his days off herds horses to save them; Jeff stores them in a horse feedlot to find them homes and save them. The drug cartel, I assume, is trying to kill us, plus they tried to steal the horses. The truck that could be involved in all of this is driven by an old man and met with a friend of ours. How much weirder can this get?" suggested Maggie.

"I am amazed by all of this. All you wanted to do was write an article about airmail arrows and fly a drone," Nan said lightly. "Look where we are now, someone has shot at us, tried to run us off the road, but for what? Wild horses that they could buy for ten dollars a head."

"You are right, there is no logic to this matter. We are acting like Nancy Drew, so maybe there is no mystery. Except drugs have flooded the area, and what better way than using horses?" sighed Maggie.

"Yeah, there is a mystery. Someone is slaughtering horses," sighed Nan.

They talked back and forth, but with no real answer, just more questions.

They pulled into Jeff's yard, he was sitting on the porch, he didn't get up when they drove in. Maggie and Nan got out of the Jeep leaving the dogs inside,

"Hi, Jeff, What is happening?" Nan shouted. No answer. Maggie felt something was wrong, as they climbed the steps, that is when they saw that Jeff had been shot right between his eyes. Maggie about barfed when she saw all the blood. They both ran down the stairs as this was a crime scene.

Nan had her phone out and was calling 911, "there has been a shooting at the Desert Rat Ranch, looks like the victim is dead." Nan answered all the dispatcher questions. After, what seemed like an hour, but was only a few minutes before the Sheriffs' cars pulled in the driveway. The ambulance was right behind them. Maggie and Nan watch everything in disbelief.

And Officer walked over to them, his name tag on his shirt, said Sgt. Anderson, "Can you tell me what happened? You are the folks that called this in, right?"

"Yes, sir, I placed the call. We found him this way when we climbed the steps," stated Nan calmly. "We didn't touch anything, I could tell he was dead by the hole between his eyes."

"Did you see anyone?" asked the officer.

"Nope, just us. We waited here for you to arrive," claimed Maggie.

The officer asked to see identification, which they gave him. He wanted to know why they were there.

"Jeff is a friend, and we came to visit," replied Nan. The officer walked off to talk to the other officer. After a few minutes, he came back and said, "you may leave, we have your information. However, we may be contacting you if we need more information."

"Thank you," they both said in unison. However, they didn't want to leave. "Officer, what about the safety of the horses?" asked Maggie.

"What do you mean?" Anderson asked.

"Well, last week, someone tried to take the fence down to steal the horses," stated Nan.

"We have had no reports on a crime out here."

"No, they didn't report it, Jeff and one of his hands stopped them, as the would-be thieves got away."

About this time, Charlie came staggering out of the big barn down by the meadow. It looked like he had been sleeping, as his clothes were all rumpled. He had a quizzical look on his face as he walked up to the Officers. "What is going on?" Then he spotted Maggie and Nan.

Maggie told him quietly that Jeff had been killed. The look on Charlie's face was pure rage, "Who would do such a thing? Jeff was the kindest man I knew."

"That is what we are going to find out," stated the Officer briskly.

Charlie was still trying to wake up, "When did this happen?"

"He was dead when we arrived about an hour ago," described Nan. "We called the Sheriff."

Anderson asked, "We would like to ask you some questions. Could I see some identification." Charlie pulled out his wallet and gave his driver's license to the Sergeant. "Did you hear any shots?"

"No, I was so tired, I had been up for over twenty-four hours, because of the horse thieves. Jeff told me he would watch and for me to get some sleep. Dang it, usually they come at dusk or later, never in the daytime."

"Why haven't you guys filed a police report about these attempted thefts?" Asked the Officer.

"What good would it do? We scared them off," said Charlie with a shrug. " I am worried about the cost of the horses, Jeff handled all of that."

"Do you have plenty of feed?" asked Nan.

"Yeah, the barn is full, probably will last a month to six weeks. Darn, who could have done this? Jeff was the kindest person I know," repeated Charlie with tears in his eyes.

"The Sheriff's Office will figure it out, I hope. Seeing you are here, we are going to head back to Carson. Give me a call later," whispered Maggie to Charlie.

"Will do." and gave them a little salute.

The CSI van drove up just then to gather evidence. The deputies had already placed tape around the porch. Maggie and Nan knew it was time for them to leave. They jumped in the Jeep and headed for home. Now the mystery had a murder.

Chapter Twenty

Maggie and Nan didn't say much on the way home. It wasn't a pleasant sight to see a murdered man. They both knew it could have been them, and they would have nightmares. "What have we got ourselves into?" asked Nan.

"Shall we step out and give what little info we have to the cops?" Asked Maggie.

They both looked at each other, "We can't," they said in unison.

Wednesday night was quilting night. Nan and Maggie went, but they were quiet. The ladies asked how things were going about the poachers.

"Not so good, someone killed Jeff," sighed Nan.

"Who would do something like that?" asked Mary.

"I assume the same people who tried to kill me," commented Maggie.

"Maybe it's time to get the Sheriff Office involved with what you know," stated Beth. "I don't want to lose you guys."

"I agree to a point, but now it is a personal matter," claimed Maggie. "However, now we have to protect ourselves and the horses."

Everyone nodded their heads as the conversation had stopped. Maggie and Nan started sewing on their quilts, drinking wine, and thinking about what had happened. The evening went slow, but Maggie got four more blocks done. Nan was about finished with her Amish quilt.

As the group was breaking up for the evening, Betty asked, "What are you going to do?"

"Not sure, but will let you know," sighed Nan.

When Maggie and Nan left the shop, they looked for the white, diesel truck, not seeing one, they drove around, but no one was following them. "Guess it is safe to go home."

When Nan got to Maggie's house, she asked, "what are we going to do?"

"Nothing, at this point. I am going to sleep on it. I haven't seen Pete to tell him the news about Jeff. Maybe he will have a suggestion," Maggie said quietly.

"You know what he is going to say. Stay out of it, let the police handle it."

"You are probably right, we will see. Talk at you tomorrow," as Maggie hopped out of the car and headed into the house with her head hung low. She was exhausted.

Thursday morning, Maggie was up and fixing coffee when Pete came into the kitchen. She poured them both a cup of coffee and placed some sweet rolls on the table.

"Why the service this morning?" queried Pete.

"We need to talk." With that, Maggie explained what had happened yesterday and asked what he thought they should do?

"What the heck. Someone killed Jeff? Darn, that is terrible." Pete rubbed his head for a minute and said, "Let's get these guys. Jeff was a nice person. Tell me everything you have found out so far."

Maggie told him about the old man and who he met at the Nugget Casino coffee shop, and that was why they went to see Jeff. Not knowing they would find Jeff shot between the eyes. Pete just looked at her in disbelief. "Do you think this woman is involved?"

"I don't know, but she has never said a word about knowing a person with a white diesel pickup. So what do you think?"

"I think we need a plan to catch a killer and stop this cartel," advised Pete. Maggie ran to retrieve her whiteboard, as the two put their heads together.

About an hour later, they had a plan. Maggie commented, "I need to tell Nan. I will have her come over. We also need to talk to Charlie." Maggie got on the phone telling Nan to come over, then she called Charlie and filled him in on the plan.

"We will catch those SOB's, come hell or high water. They came back last night. This time I shot at them. Don't think I hit anybody, but scared them off," snarled Charlie.

Maggie asked if he knew the woman, and she described her. But he said he didn't know her. Jeff might have, as he was the one that went to town most of the time. They all felt good about the plan, as at least they had something to work with.

The next couple of days, Maggie worked on her new book. She had interviewed an interesting lady with lots of history about Nevada. Nan came over to visit. "Haven't seen or heard from you, what is going on?"

"Nothing, just working on the new book. I have to keep my brain busy. Should be hearing back from the Beta readers on my airmail story".

"Well, we have that party to go to this weekend. What are you bringing?"

"Darn, that is tomorrow night, and I have my class reunion on Sunday. Can you believe I have been out of school for fifty years? I am curious to see what everyone looks like now that we are old," as Maggie made a face. Nan laughed. "Mine will be next year."

Maggie poured them each a glass of wine, and they talked about their plan. "What do you think she will say when we confront her?" Asked Nan.

"I thought about having a Sheriff Deputy waiting outside, but what if we're wrong?" replied Maggie. "However, she does know where I live, and she does shoot. I am so confused I just can't believe it's might be her."

"I know. She is such a quiet thing," stated Nan.

"You know what they say *still water runs deep*," sighs Maggie. "But we will find out soon enough."

Maggie was glad when Wednesday came, and she would get back to working on her quilt block, which would keep her mind busy. Maggie and Nan came bouncing in, like always, with a good bottle of wine.

Everybody started talking at once to see what they found out this last week. Maggie replied, "Nothing. I worked on my new book." And she sat down with her blanket project. Everybody just looked at her with quizzical looks.

After the wine was poured, Mary very soft-spoken as she was, said, "I have something to tell you all. I have been seeing an older man for several months."

Everybody starts saying, "What???"

"His name is Matt Sorenson, he is a widow too. The best part is he has asked me to marry him. I have told him yes. Would you gals help me with the wedding?" stammered Mary.

Everyone jumped up and hug her. "We would be thrilled. In fact, we could have the wedding at my new shop in Gardnerville. It has a back parking lot big enough for a great party."

"What is this? A night of surprises. Mary is getting married, and Beth bought a new store. Wow!" shouted Nan, looking at Maggie with an oh shit look.

"Mary, are you aware Matt drives a white dodge diesel truck with cattle guards on it and his plate are part of the group we have been staking out? Asked Maggie.

Mary put her hand to her mouth, "No. I have never seen Matt's vehicle. We always meet somewhere. You don't think he's involved with the horse poaching?" Mary was quite stressed now.

Nan jumped in, "No. We don't think he is involved, as he is on a cane. However, we wanted you to know he was a suspect. We got the information on the trucks from you, in fact."

Mary was quite upset, said very quietly, "Matt wouldn't hurt a fly, he is a sweet man who lost his wife, Ace, a few years ago."

"Sorry, Mary, to tell you that news," sighed Maggie.

"That's okay, I needed to know. But he lives alone, or so he says. He is too crippled to chase horses, and Matt is not rich enough to be selling dope. I just can't believe he would do anything like that or hire someone to do it." as Mary rubs her head in disbelief.

"I think you are right, but Nan and I have to go back to the drawing board to see who is behind all of this," replied Maggie.

Beth chimed in with a big smile, "We will plan the wedding here, just tells us when."

Everyone said, "We will help."

Betty spoke up and said, "I know a cake baker. We are set."

"Thank you so much for your support. I really do care for this man. I have lived alone for so long, it will be nice to have a partner. Someone to cook for and argue with," laughed Mary.

The night ended early after the big news, no one did much quilting. On the way home, Nan and Maggie discussed what they were going to do.   Maggie said, "I am going to go over and see Charlie tomorrow to see if he has any ideas want to come?"

"Sure, I have nothing going on, pick me up around nine, if that's okay?"

"Sounds good, see you then," as Maggie dropped Nan at her house. She couldn't wait to tell Pete the big news.

Chapter Twenty-One

When Maggie got home, she went into Pete's office to tell him the latest. "Hey, Hon, you are not going to believe what happened tonight?"

"You finished your quilt," he said jokingly.

"Not even. Didn't even get a block done. Mary announced tonight she is getting married to the gent in the white diesel pickup that lives up Six-Mile canyon." Replied Maggie out of breath. "Can you believe it? The bad part was we thought she was involved. What kind of friend am I to suspect her, but darn, she fitted the bill. Knew where I live, and shoots in the Police Olympics."

"Wow. Getting married to the guy. That is good news for her, Bob has been dead now, what six years? But, you were right, she did fit the bill. What are you planning now?"

"Well, Nan and I were thinking of going over to see Charlie tomorrow to see if he has some ideas. Want to come with us?

"Sorry. Can't have another darn meeting in Reno, but keep me informed," stated Pete. "Can't believe Mary is getting married."

"Plus the other news is Beth bought a building in Gardnerville and is moving her shop. She offered the backyard of the new place for the wedding. We are all helping Mary with this event." Maggie said as she left the office.

At nine, Maggie was at Nan's house, tooting the horn for her and Shep. Yazoo started his little wine when he saw Shep. "Shep is coming Yazoo, be patience."

"Good morning, you two, ready for a ride?" asked Maggie.

"I brought sweet rolls and coffee," commented Nan.

"You are so organized, thank you. I did grab a cup of coffee this morning, but didn't eat," reported Maggie.

They talked about what happened last night. "Thank goodness I didn't invite a cop. That would have been so embarrassing or all of us," stammered Maggie.

"Yes, we would have been the talk of the town for a while," laughed Nan.

The rest of the trip, they talked about what they were going to say to Charlie and see what he thought. Maggie had Nan tried to reach Charlie to let him know they were coming over, no answer, and his mailbox was full. Plus, they also wanted to know when Jeff was going to be buried.

Pulling up to the ranch, Maggie noticed some horses were missing, in fact, a whole bunch. "Nan, do you notice some of the horses are gone."

"Yeah. Plus, I don't see anybody around. Wonder what is going on?"

Maggie parked the Jeep up by the house, getting out, she told, "Yazoo, you stay," but left the Jeep door open. Nan did the same, but closed her door. Maggie walked up to the front door, it was locked. "It's locked, that's funny. Wonder where Charlie has wandered off too." Maggie tried his cell, still no answer. "Now, I am concerned. Think I will call the cops just in case he is dead in the barn. I do not want to find another dead body."

Maggie no sooner got off her cell when she saw a white pickup coming down the road and turning into the ranch. She saw that Charlie was driving an there were two men with him. Maggie recognized them as the men who tried to run them off the road. Not knowing what to expect, she unbuckled her Glock on her hip under her blouse. "Nan, stay close to the Jeep, I don't like what I see."

The white Dodge truck pulled up, blocking the Jeep, and Charlie got out. The two men stayed in the truck. Charlie walked over with a big smile, "Didn't expect to see you guys. What is going on?"

"That's what I like to know? I see horses are missing," spat Maggie.

"Yes, I am moving them to a different ranch, don't have enough hands to keep the thieves away." Turning up into the driveway was a cattle truck, this one was different than the one they used before. Maggie thought, *Crap, there are four of them,* as the two men got out of the truck and one had a rifle. "Bruno, it's okay," stated Charlie, "They are not thieves."

"No, but I'm figuring you are. Why Charlie? I thought you cared about the horses and Jeff?"

"Damn. I knew you were going to be a problem, you're like a dog with a bone. I wanted this to go down differently," smirk Charlie. "You're like Jeff, so righteous. He started to suspect me when he saw the truck. I tried to explain, but he fired me."

"Again, why? Was it the money? Maggie asked as she backed closer to the Jeep. She needed time before the cops got there.

"I guess it doesn't matter what I tell you, you'll never be able to tell anyone. Darn right, it was about the money. Each horse can pack over a hundred thousand dollars worth of drugs. Take that times a hundred plus horses, I can live in South America as a king."

Maggie notice Bruno had the rifle half-ass pointed at her, just waiting for Charlie's signal. Maggie whispered into the Jeep, "fetch" and out jumped an eighty-pound dog dropping Bruno to the ground, grabbing the rifle and placing it by Maggie's feet before anyone knew what happened. Maggie had drawn her Glock and said, "Now let's be calm until the police get here."

The guy in the cattle truck started backing down the road. Charlie just smiled, "There are still three of us, you can't get us all."

"True, I only have to shoot you first," snarled Maggie.

The smile left Charlie's face as he charged at her. Maggie fired, shooting him in the knee. Charlie screamed in pain as his knee cap was blown away. "You shot me," he shouted.

Quickly, she pointed her gun on the other two, 'You want some of this?" Yazoo has his teeth showing. Nan ran in front of the Jeep. The men backed up closer to their truck. Everyone was safe except Charlie, who rolled on the ground in pain. Maggie saw the police car coming up the road. Thank goodness this adventure was over.

Maggie filled out all the paperwork. The Sheriff had called for an ambulance for Charlie. She wasn't sure what was going to happen to the twenty or thirty horses left, but she had an idea.

She called Mary and asked, "Seeing Matt has some acreage, do you think he would want to board about thirty horses until we find them homes?"

Mary said, "I will call him, but don't think there will be a problem." Maggie thought *Pete might know of someone who could transport them.*

After about an hour, they let Nan and Maggie go, but not without a lecture. The Sargeant told them they could have been killed. Bruno and Mac both had warrants out on them for assault, robbery, and drugs. The rifle was the same caliber that killed Jeff. Also, it may be the same gun used when they tried to kill her. Forensics would check on all of that.

Maggie gave Yazoo a big hug. Nan said, "I didn't know he was police trained. "

"He's not. He is trained to fetch sticks. He just thought the rifle was a big stick, and I got lucky. But let me tell you, I almost peed my pants when I shot Charlie, what if I had missed."

"I don't know about you, but I could use a drink right now. Let's find the nearest watering hole. What a story we have to tell. However, I am sorry that some of the horses couldn't be saved."

Chapter Twenty-Two

Wednesday night quilting class, nothing got done, the wine flowed Nan, and Maggie told everybody all the details of the capture of Charlie. Nan said, "You know we couldn't have done any of this if it weren't for you guys."

Maggie gave them all a big clap, saying, "Thanks to you, we put a hole in one of those drug cartels."

Betty chimed in, "Now let's plan a wedding at the new Fabric Chic's in Gardnerville for Mary and Matt."

"Hear, hear," they all said as they toasted their wine glasses.

Maggie was excited she finished the rewrites on the airmail arrows for the Nevada Magazine. Now it's up to the editor. They replied quickly, saying they liked it just the way it was written, and it would be in either the September or the October issue. Her new book was going to the beta readers and should be out by the Candy Dance in Genoa, which is the end of September. Pete was getting ready for the State 4H shoot in Las Vegas in Oct. Overall, life was back to normal in the McDonald household, except for mastering that darn drone. Maggie thought, *and it looks like the quilt will be a Christmas present for her daughter next year.*

Made in the USA
Columbia, SC
24 April 2022

59381243R00091